A Gunslinger for Grace

SARAH LAMB

Thank you for being
part of my group!

Sarah Lamb

Contents

To Patricia, for being a wonderful friend, neighbor, and support. I'm so glad to know you!

Chapter 1

1875, Kansas

A sudden crash startled Grace Fletcher. She sat up in bed, then sprang forward, wrapping her robe around her. "I'll get you this time," she muttered, and flung open her bedroom door. Without a thought to her safety, she unlatched the door leading down the stairs and to the general store that she managed solely on her own since her husband's passing three years prior.

"Who's there?" she called out. "I've sent for the sheriff."

That was a lie, though whoever was there wouldn't know that. But just like every other time before, there wasn't anyone there by the time she stepped into the shop. Only a mess. This time, a glass jar of penny candy was broken, along with the globe on the oil lamp she kept near the counter. Surprisingly, the oil hadn't spilled.

Luckily, she'd kept the money in the safe. The safe which no one, no one at all, had the combination for. She'd seen to that.

Over the last several months, there had been multiple instances where her store was broken into. Money was taken at first, until she made use of the safe she special ordered. Now, it was more often than not small objects taken, things easily put into a pocket, or things damaged for whatever terrible reason the criminal had.

The problem was that she wasn't sure who was breaking into her store—or why. The sheriff had promised to keep his men nearby and set up a nighttime patrol, and she reported each incident, but never had she, or the sheriff's men, found out who was breaking into her store.

This was one problem that she didn't need, on top of her other problems. It was hard enough being a woman alone, trying to manage both the raising of her children and running a store to support her family. To top it off, motherhood was being less than rewarding as of late. Her two children, Alice and Calvin, had been rebelling and her exhaustion at trying to keep them safe and behaving, combined with the store's constant destruction, might just do her in.

At first, Grace thought their acting out was simply the grief of losing their father three years before to the sickness that took nearly a quarter of the town. Both children had been very close to their father. They adored him, and his passing was both sudden and frightening. Grace herself had struggled deeply with it.

However, as time passed, she realized that the way they were acting was more serious than that. Their behavior was reckless, and she was at a loss to put a stop to it.

Alice was too interested in men. Not boys her age, which was thirteen, but those much older. Meanwhile, Calvin was roaming around with other eleven-year-olds, getting into as much trouble as he could, even skipping school or staying out after dark at times.

Both were experts at sneaking out of the house and, to be honest, as she was so busy trying to run the store on her own to keep a roof over their heads and food in their stomachs, it was quite possible she was missing quite a bit of their behavior.

The problem was how to rein them in. She just wasn't sure how. That stress, combined with her worry over the store break-ins was the final straw. She was sure of it. Grace honestly wasn't sure how much longer she could manage everything on her own.

Grace sighed, wrapped her robe a little tighter around her, and headed back toward the stairs. She'd have to clean up the mess tomorrow. It was too late now, it was near midnight, and she wanted to get some sleep before making breakfast and getting the children ready for school.

What she needed was a solution to her problems. But...what could that be? She trudged up the steps and stopped. Was that a light under Calvin's door? She hesitated, her hand on the knob, then gave in and turned it, pushing the door open.

When her head poked through the door, it was dark inside. Calvin was in his bed, but there was the smell of a recently extinguished lamp. She moved closer, resting her hand on his head. He seemed to be asleep, but she wasn't fooled. He'd been out somewhere, she was sure of it. His forehead was damp, his breathing wasn't even, and his eyes were squeezed closed just a little too tight.

Sighing, Grace left the room. All of a sudden, she wasn't in a hurry to get back to bed. It meant tomorrow, and all its problems, would arrive just a little too soon.

Chapter 2

Grace closed her eyes for a moment, took a slow, deep breath, then reopened them. "I apologize, Mrs. Martin," she said, and reached into the cash register. She handed over some coins. "I hope this will be enough to pay for your ruined laundry."

The other woman took the coins, nodded, but then sniffed, "You need to keep a better eye on your children, Ms. Fletcher. That boy of yours is always up to no good. It won't be a surprise to me if he ends up on one of those wanted posters at the sheriff's office one day."

Grace's eyes pricked with tears of both anger and despair as the woman turned. Didn't anyone see that she was doing the best she could? Of course not. They only complained she wasn't doing enough when something happened. It was tempting to just leave. Sell the store and move on, take her children away from the vices they seemed drawn to. But she couldn't. What would she do? Where would she go? Would trouble just find the children again? Probably. Older men and troublemakers were everywhere.

The door's chime sounded as Mrs. Martin left. Grace sighed and turned to the newspaper sitting in front of her. She scanned the headlines, then the ads. Perhaps there was someone nearby looking for work. Another pair of hands in the store wouldn't be bad. In fact, it might be just enough to help her breathe a little easier. She could afford to pay someone for a while.

After a few moments of reading the paper, she frowned and folded it back up. Nothing. Someone walked in, and she looked up, smiling.

"Becky!" Her dearest friend, and the pastor's wife, walked in, her own smile bright. Just the sight of it made Grace feel better. Becky never judged her, she was like a soothing balm on a wound, and right now, that's what she needed.

"How are you, Grace dear?" she asked as she stepped up to the counter.

"I'm praying for an answer," Grace admitted.

Her friend reached over and squeezed her hand gently, then released it. "What's happened?"

A tear of frustration escaped, and Grace angrily brushed it away. "My store was broken into again last night. If this keeps going, I'm not sure I'll be able to stay open. It's gotten where the expense of repairs and damaged goods is quite significant."

Becky looked concerned. "Oh Grace, I'm so sorry. I can't believe the criminal hasn't been caught yet." Her voice was filled with compassion. "You've been through so much the last few years. It's too much for one person to manage on their own."

Both women were quiet for a moment, then Becky asked suddenly, "Have you looked about hiring someone to help you here? To keep an eye on things?"

"I have," Grace said with a nod. She tapped the newspaper on the shop counter. "I was just looking at the ads placed. However, there's nothing for anyone looking for work."

"Then why not make your own advertisement?" Becky suggested. "Sometimes we must make our own way when one doesn't exist."

"My own?" Grace paused. She'd not thought of that. "What a simple solution. I cannot believe I didn't think of that sooner. You are right. Wasn't that the sermon on Sunday?" She gave a wry laugh and shook her head. "I'm so glad you walked in today. You are truly the answer to a prayer."

Becky smiled in return. "Good. I hope that someone answers, and answers soon. Well, I can't stay any longer. I just felt like I should come over and see you. I'm so glad I did. Best of luck, Grace. Do let me know if I can help you somehow."

"Thank you, Becky," Grace nodded, and then waved as her friend left. The door had hardly closed behind her when she already had a pencil and a slip of paper in her hand. "How to word this..."

After a moment of thinking, she started to scratch away on the paper, then leaned back in satisfaction. "Yes. This will do."

Her ad read: *Wanted. A man to help prevent thefts in my store and to assist with other small tasks. Room and board included, and a modest salary.*

Would anyone answer? She hoped someone would. Grace went to the front door, placed a sign notifying that she'd be right back, locked it behind her, and then scurried over to the newspaper office.

The small building, not more than two tiny rooms, was tucked between the post office and the bank. Their town wasn't the most robust in size, containing only a single main street, but there certainly was enough trouble for her son to find, she thought, pressing her lips together as she glanced toward the schoolhouse.

Grace pushed open the door to the newspaper office and went in. "Hello," she greeted Mr. Mason, the owner of the paper. "I'd like to place an ad, please."

He took the paper from her and read it. "Might get a few more responses if you send it around to a few papers," he suggested. "Happy to do that for you. Will cost a little extra though."

"No, I agree," Grace said. "Can you do that for me?" She reached a hand into her purse. "How much?"

He rubbed his chin. "Two dollars ought to do it," he said. "Put it in a half dozen papers."

Grace slid the money across the counter to him. "Thank you. When can I expect it to run?"

"Give it a week," Mr. Mason told her as he put the money into a small wooden box. "It will be in our next paper. I'll telegraph it over to the other papers right away, just as soon as you leave."

A rush of gratitude flooded Grace. A weight seemed to lift. Help could be as soon as only a week away.

"Thank you," she repeated, and left the newspaper office. As the door closed behind her, she couldn't help but feel relieved. It seemed almost symbolic. The door closing on her troubles. As she unlocked and then opened her shop door, she smiled. *Yes, and a new door opening.*

Her heart felt lighter that day. In fact, everything seemed to be going well. Alice only talked about the girls at school, none of the boys, Calvin returned with good marks on an essay he'd written, and dinner was a quiet affair. If only it would last!

As she tucked the children into bed, Grace was relieved when they seemed to stay there visiting dreamland, at least as far as she could tell.

For herself, she tried to rest, but her mind wouldn't still. Though she was relieved she might get some help at the store, that also opened up a worry. What sort of person would answer the ad, she wondered. Hopefully, it would be someone who was strong enough to help lift the heavy sacks of flour and oats and beans that she got monthly. Maybe it would be an older man, someone without a family, who just needed to stay busy.

Perhaps it would be a Godly man, one who could be a good influence on Alice and Calvin. That thought made her smile. Yes, that's just what she needed. Someone who would set a good example for her children.

Slipping out of bed, she checked, as she'd become accustomed to as of late, on her store downstairs. Everything seemed in order. She went back up and peered in at the children once more. Both were sleeping soundly. She could tell it was genuine.

Grace returned to her own bed. The last thought she had before slipping into a sound sleep was it was remarkable how life changing one small action, such as placing an advertisement could be.

A week felt a long time to wait for her ad to appear, but when it did, she was sure the answer to all her prayers would arrive. The thought left a smile on her face as she slept.

Chapter 3

"Another good job, James. Thank you," the sheriff said, as he hauled the rustler into the jail cell.

"Happy to help," James Clark answered, accepting the reward money the deputy handed him. Off in the distance, the coach he'd arrived in with his bounty drove off. "I thought it was a just dessert. The stagecoach robber riding to jail in the coach he failed to rob."

The men laughed at the irony. James's eye fell on the newspaper. "Anything good in there?" he asked, with a nod of his head at it. "Could use another job."

"Not much in there right now," the deputy said. He slid the paper closer. "Pretty quiet right now. No criminals nearby that I know of. Take a look through if you want. We're done with it. You are welcome to the paper."

"I will," he remarked, and tipped his hat. "Thank you, Sheriff."

Stepping out into the street, James made his way over to the bank. He waited a few moments for his turn, then stepped to the counter. "I want to send this," he said, and pushed a paper across the counter, along with half of his reward money.

The teller nodded. "I'll make your deposit, and send a telegram on your behalf. Do you want to add anything more to it?" He held a pencil poised over a notepad.

"Nah," James said. "She'll know who it's from." He collected the receipt and left. That ought to tide Jenny over for a while. He never told her he sent her money, and she never asked who sent it. They both knew, and that was good enough for them.

He couldn't stand to watch her suffer. Half of what he made got sent to her, and hopefully by the end of the year she'd be in a much better position. It was all he could do, and why he often took dangerous jobs.

James settled onto a bench and opened the paper, letting his eyes drift over each advertisement. It seemed pretty quiet in this area. No escaped criminals, no wanted notices.

No work.

A groan escaped. He was stuck here too, unless he bought a horse, since he'd boarded his to get on that stagecoach to catch the thief. He had enough reward money to do that, or take a coach back to his horse, but something about the idea wasn't appealing. Not yet. Not until he got desperate. That was a lot of money he'd just worked for, to throw it away on buying a horse he'd just have to sell.

To top it off, he was a little tired, and maybe if he hung around for a little while, something would open up that would send him back where he'd come from—and with an even fuller pocket. It had happened before. A little patience just might be in order, that's all.

He frowned. But where else to look? Maybe he could ask around at the post office. There could be some wanted posters not out yet, or a dispute on a ranch that needed handling. It seemed like a good plan. James shook the newspaper and started to fold it when a word caught his eye. *Thefts.*

Well now, this might be something. He squinted and read the advertisement closer.

Wanted. A man to help prevent thefts in my store, and to assist with other small tasks. Room and board included, and a modest salary.

James rubbed one hand over his chin while he thought. It wasn't his usual work, but it also didn't sound too hard. This might just be the perfect thing to tide him over until a big job came along. Even better, he wouldn't have to pay for his bed or his meals. That would save him a lot of money while he waited for something better.

Deciding to learn more, James stood and made his way back to the sheriff's office. The sheriff and his deputy looked up as he walked in.

"Didn't expect to see you again so soon," the sheriff said.

"Didn't think I'd be back so quick," James agreed. He opened the newspaper to the notice and placed it on the desk in front of him. "What can you tell me about this ad?" James asked, tapping on it.

The sheriff leaned close to see it, then leaned back with a grunt. "That would be Mrs. Fletcher. She owns the general store." He shook his head. "The last few years have been pretty bad for her."

James raised his eyebrows. "Oh?" He didn't miss the twinge of regret in the other man's voice.

"Husband passed away," the sheriff said, "and her two kids started to get wild. Her son especially is a problem. He's been running in a pack with some troublemakers. They vandalize before school, after school, even during school. No matter how many times they get caught, they don't stop."

James nodded. He knew the type. That was him, before he'd been set straight.

"Not entirely her fault," the sheriff continued. "She's a good woman, but she can only do so much, running that store, taking care of her kids. Now, the last few months, someone's been breaking into her store."

"And you've not caught them?" James couldn't help but feel surprised. Theft wasn't looked on kindly by anyone and in a small town like this, it seemed that there wouldn't be too much else this serious to keep the sheriff occupied.

The deputy broke in then. "We've tried. Had men stationed, keep an eye on the place, even stop by a few times a night, but it still happens. Her front glass window was broken last week. She's got a safe now, so her money isn't stolen now like it had been, but a few nights ago, someone busted one of the smaller windows in the back of the store. Messed the place up. She's about at her wit's end."

"So, she's looking for a man to help, and maybe stop the thieving?" James asked. He tucked his thumbs into his waistband. This didn't sound too bad. Often, just having a man around stopped problems like that, especially if the thief was someone who knew this Mrs. Fletcher lived alone without a way to defend herself and her own.

"Yep. You thinking of applying?" The sheriff looked hopeful. "You'd be an asset to her. I'll vouch for your character."

James rubbed at his jaw. It felt a little scratchy. He still wasn't used to the short beard he was growing, but he was hoping to make himself look a little older. He had his mama's baby face, and not many would believe he was a man of thirty-five. It came in handy, he got underestimated at times, but others it worked against him. Finally, he answered, "I might. Something different to do for a little while."

The sheriff stood a little taller. "Would be a great help to us," he admitted. "We can't catch the person. And Mrs. Fletcher sure needs the help."

"Why hasn't she remarried?" James asked, curiously. "Wouldn't that fix her problem? A father for her children to keep them in line and a man to do the heavy work around the store?"

The deputy laughed. "Sure it would, but we men are outnumbered in this town. Why, I have four daughters myself and no sons. Must be something in the water! Not enough men to go around."

James laughed too. He hadn't expected that answer. Usually, the problem was the opposite out here in the West. He took the newspaper up again. "I'll just stop by and talk with her. See what she says. That store there?" he asked, pointing to the good-sized building nestled between a dentist and the barber.

"That's it," the sheriff agreed. "I'll stop by later and put in a good word if you need it."

Waving his thanks, James set out across the street. He wondered what this Mrs. Fletcher was like. Probably old. Gray hair. Stooped over, maybe. He could help the old woman out for a while. Do a good deed. Send some more money to Jenny, all while getting a few good homecooked meals. He patted his stomach. Truth be told, that was what was appealing to him the most about this potential arrangement. Meals and a bed.

He stepped up to the store, his eyes taking in the new window. The putty didn't yet seem dry, and a new sign hadn't been painted on it proclaiming that this was the mercantile. His eyes fell to the door, where scuff marks around the lock showed someone had tried to force it, likely multiple times.

James shook his head. He didn't abide by thieves. You never knew what kind of effect your actions had on another when stealing, but it was never good.

He pushed open the door and walked in. As his eyes sought for the front counter, he stopped in surprise. A tired looking woman stood behind the counter, a girl of maybe twelve or thirteen next to her. It was obvious they were mother and daughter. But the mother...

Soft blonde hair was pinned up on her head. Her dress was of a cornflower blue that complimented her creamy skin perfectly, and amber eyes, filled with worry, met his.

James felt his heart start to hammer and almost stumbled. His mouth felt dry and his tongue froze. Mrs. Fletcher wasn't what he had thought she'd be. Not at all.

Chapter 4

Grace bit her lip as she bent over the store ledger. "Alice, can you please add these numbers up for me?"

"Sure." Alice came over and quickly tallied the numbers.

For all the problems Alice gave her with being overly interested in men at such a young age, she was grateful that otherwise, her daughter was a sweet girl, and helpful. Alice helped often in the store, usually after school, and Grace just didn't know what she'd do without her assistance.

Seeing the total her daughter displayed, Grace's shoulders slumped. She hadn't added wrong. Nearly seventy-five dollars of things were stolen or broken that month. If this kept going, she would be in serious financial trouble. It had also been more than a week since she'd placed the ad for help. Every day she grew more discouraged that no one had contacted her. She was about ready to crawl back into bed and stay there.

"I'm sorry, Mama," Alice said. "Maybe the sheriff will catch them."

"I'm giving up hope on that. They haven't yet. Whoever it is, they are just too clever to be caught." Grace sighed, even though she felt like screaming. "But I just don't understand. Why is it always my store?"

"It's not just you," Alice said, shaking her head. "Over at the shoemaker, he's had things damaged too."

"Oh? Did you hear that from someone?" Grace glanced out the window toward the shoemaker and wondered who else might be prey to the thieves.

"Marty Smith told me," Alice said, unable to keep the giggle out of her voice.

"Marty Smith?" Grace narrowed her eyes. "Alice, you are too young to be talking to him. He's nearly twice your age."

"I'm mature for my age," Alice said, scowling as she crossed her arms. "Everyone says so. Especially Marty." She giggled again as a silly expression came over her face.

"And if Marty told you the sky was green, would you believe that too?" Grace asked.

Alice walked over to the shop window and peered at the sky. "Is it? Are we expecting a storm? The sky looks blue to me, right now."

Grace just shook her head. "Never mind. Just stay away from him, please?"

When Alice didn't answer, Grace gritted her teeth. "I'm just—"

"Trying to protect me. I know. But I don't need protecting. If anything, it's Calvin who needs protecting—from himself. He and those other boys are always up to no good." Alice crossed her arms and walked back over to the counter. "He's the one who needs to behave."

"I agree," Grace said. "But I'm—"

Just then, the door opened, and a stranger walked in. Alice turned away, gathering her schoolbooks. "See you later," she said.

"Goodbye, dear," Grace said. Then, to the stranger, "Hello, how can I help you?"

The man didn't answer at first, just gave a slow look around the store before turning his cool gaze to her. "Actually, I might be able to help you."

"Oh?" Grace asked.

"Yes. Forgive me for being so forward, but I saw your ad and wanted to answer in person since I was passing through. I thought I might be able to assist. You were looking for help in your store?"

Grace studied the stranger for a long moment. He was tall, looked fairly young, but there was something in his eyes that showed he was serious about the offer. The question was, why had he answered her ad? He didn't seem at all what she'd imagined a man accepting her poor paying offer would be. No, this man looked able-bodied, in his prime, and not the sort to want to work in a shop like hers. And Alice...once Alice saw him, she'd be mooning over him in a way Grace didn't want to deal with.

It was on the tip of her tongue to tell him no thank you, but then she stopped. She could use some help, and no one else had answered. Having a man around would possibly put a stop to the destructive acts in the store. It also would be nice to have someone help with some of the store's chores. Maybe, just maybe, he could even help her with calming Calvin down, if he set a good example.

Making up her mind to at least speak with him a little more, she asked, "Is that so? I admit, Mr..."

"Clark. James Clark," he said, tipping his hat.

"Mr. Clark, I could use a little help, but I also have two children, both quite impressionable, who are my responsibility to keep safe."

"And you are worried that I am of a questionable character?"

His comment made her pause. Did she? Help needed or not, he was a stranger. Would she be inviting more trouble in by offering him the job? It wouldn't be too late to tell him the position was filled.

"Mr. Clark, I—"

"Am a widow, with two children she wants to protect. I understand that," he said, his eyes honest and clear. "I fault you none for that. However, I don't mean you or your children any harm."

"How-how did you know I was a widow?" Grace stammered.

He gave her an odd look. "Ma'am, forgive me for saying so, but it was pretty clear from your ad. You need a man to help around the place and you've got someone stealing from your store. If you were married, you'd have the man to help and a thief deterrent. You also mentioned your children. If you had a husband, you also wouldn't be concerned about their behavior or having me around."

Grace was nearly speechless. Who was this man? He seemed incredibly observant.

"Let's be honest with each other," he continued. "You've got trouble and need some help. I was looking for a job for a little while. Yours interests me. It's been a while since I've had a job that didn't require me to be shot at. Homecooked meals added on is also mighty tempting."

Two of the words leaped out at Grace and stuck in her mind, filling her with worry. "Shot at?" Grace stared at him. "What kind of jobs have you had before now?"

"I didn't mention?" He grinned and tipped his hat up a little. "I'm a gunslinger."

Chapter 5

James dropped his bag in a back room of the store and looked around. There was a small straw-filled mattress with a down pillow and two blankets, an empty chest, and a small chair. Some pegs on the wall completed the room. It wasn't much, but he was just fine with it.

A smile teased at his lips as he thought about Mrs. Fletcher's expression when he'd told her he was a gunslinger. Likely she'd expected a rough mannered individual who would spit on her floors. Maybe pull out his gun and practice his aim on her jars of preserves. It was a reaction most respectable women had.

He didn't blame her, really. A lot of gunslingers didn't have the best of manners. He took pride in the fact that he was a little different from most. After all, it was true. His gunslinging was in part necessity. It was just lucky he also happened to be quite skilled at it.

Just after he'd told her his profession, the sheriff walked in and vouched for him, and let her know he'd brought several men in for justice for them and was on the right side of the law, not just a gun for hire. That seemed to set her mind at ease.

Leaving his room, he looked for her and soon found himself at work unloading a wagon filled with crates of goods. He had the good fortune of starting work on the day of the month she got most of her deliveries.

As usual, he had great timing.

"New here?" the driver asked, squinting at him before taking a bite out of a jerky stick.

"Yup." James grunted, lifting a particularly heavy crate marked fragile. He teetered into the back storage room.

"I'll give you some advice," the driver said when James came back outside. "No charge."

James wiped his sleeve across his forehead and took a drink of water from a jug at the back door. "What's that?"

"Watch out for the boy. Mrs. Fletcher's just fine, her girl Alice is too, but that boy, he's a troublemaker if there ever was one. He and those other boys he hangs around with unhitched my wagon the other day and made me late for a delivery. Few days before that, they threw mud all over the laundry that Mrs. Martin takes in for the town. No good, that boy."

"Probably just needs to settle down," James said. "All boys can be a little wild."

"This is more than wild," the driver said, as James grabbed the last crate. "This is downright heading for trouble. The kind that's at the end of a barrel."

James watched in surprise as the wagon driver jumped into the seat and drove off. As he stared at the puffs of dust rising from the wagon wheels, he wondered, was the boy really that bad? The sheriff had mentioned something about him too. He'd not met him yet, but unless the kid was doing really terrible things, he couldn't see how any boy of Grace Fletcher's could be fixing for a future staring down the end of a barrel.

She seemed a caring mother who was making herself exhausted trying to take care of everything. In fact, though he'd hardly been there, he felt a pang of sympathy when he thought about that. Life in the West was hard enough, but to be a woman alone, that was even harder. Every woman deserved a man to protect her when she needed it, and to care for her so she didn't have to look so worn down. It made him wonder how much of that her children caused.

He lifted a sack he'd rested by the back door and carried it in. James knew all about boys who got themselves into the kind of trouble that had dangerous and even deadly results. He'd almost been there himself.

In fact, it was those very things he'd done as a child that made him so good at his job now. He knew how troublemakers and outlaws thought, and could often stay a step ahead of them.

Inside the store, he could hear Mrs. Fletcher talking to a woman. He snuck a peek at her, then went back out. There was supposed to be one more delivery he was supposed to keep an eye out for.

James settled himself on a barrel as he waited, allowing himself a moment's rest. Mrs. Fletcher might just be the prettiest woman he'd ever seen. He wondered how she'd look without those worry lines around her eyes, or the tightness in her lips. Lips that lush were meant for smiles. For kisses. Not strain.

What was her smile like? It was obvious the last few years had been difficult for her. He wondered when the last time was she'd laughed. Or slept. She looked exhausted. It made him determined to help as much as he could until it was time for him to move on. Maybe he'd even catch that crook upsetting her. For her sake, he was going to try. Maybe just word going around town that she now had a hired man would be enough to stop the person.

A loaded wagon pulled up, and a man jumped down. "I'm here for the delivery," he said. "You unloading?"

"Sure am," James said. "Let me just let Mrs. Fletcher know you are here in case she needed to talk to you."

He turned to walk in. He wasn't looking forward to unloading those heavy sacks, but the idea that the store was closing for the day soon, and he'd be sitting down for a hot meal near a beautiful woman, would lighten the load.

He opened the door and walked in, looking for Mrs. Fletcher. Too bad he never stayed in one place for very long. Mrs. Fletcher was one fine woman, and he'd like to get to know her much better.

Chapter 6

"A gunslinger. The man's a gunslinger, and you hired him?" Becky stared at her, a look of absolute shock on her face. Grace understood. She'd worn that same expression only hours before.

Taking a deep breath, she said, "I spoke with the sheriff about him. He told me he wasn't wanted, not that he knew of. He's brought in several men to them before. He doesn't pass this way often, but since he arrived...well, I've not had anyone else offer. I'm getting desperate."

Grace knew she was stumbling with her words and that, even to her own ears, her excuses might sound thin, but one thing was true. She was desperate. If only Becky would understand. She needed at least one person who didn't think poorly of her for doing what she had to do.

"But your children! And you, a woman alone..." Becky shook her head as her voice trailed off. "Grace, I do declare you aren't thinking. All those sleepless nights have caught up to you and addled your brain."

"Oddly enough," Grace said, "I feel at peace with the decision. You know, maybe he's just who I need to keep the store safe. And Calvin out of trouble. If nothing else, he's a help for the store, which is something you know how much I need. Today is delivery day. All those crates and sacks...I just can't do it, Becky."

Becky opened her mouth, then closed it again. A thoughtful expression came over her face and she nodded slowly. "You know, you might just be right. Not just for helping you with the heavy work in the store. A man like that is good at stopping trouble. Sometimes before it even starts."

With a small smile, Grace nodded. "That's what I'm hoping. He's—" she broke off as the gunslinger entered the shop.

"The miller is here, ma'am," he told her. "I'll just unload the wagon in the rear storage room."

"That you," Grace said. She turned back to Becky, who was staring wide-eyed.

"Oh my! You neglected to say how handsome he is," the pastor's wife breathed.

Grace laughed, then she considered her friend's words. He was handsome, in a way. She'd not really paid much attention before, but he had a strong jaw, a nicely shaped nose, and an open honesty on his face. It seemed quite the contrast to his background.

She wondered how a man that attractive didn't already have a wife. Was he not looking for one? Or was it because he had a dangerous profession and didn't want to put one in danger? For some reason, the question made her curious to learn more about him. Why did he do what he did?

Becky's voice brought her back to the present. Grace was almost embarrassed at how quickly her thoughts had been filled with a man she hardly knew. It was lack of sleep; that must be it.

"Well, I have to be going," Becky said. She leaned in closer, her voice dropping, "I want to hear all about him later. Don't leave *anything* out." Becky straightened then, and reached to squeeze her friend's hand. "And, Grace, good luck. I hope it works out for you."

Grace waved goodbye and returned to the order she was placing from the catalog for canning jars and wax for sealing them. Carefully, she finished filling out the order form, then set it aside to take over to the post office in the morning.

In the distance, the school bell rang. Alice and Calvin would be along soon. She realized she'd need to make introductions to Mr. Clark. Should she tell them about the fact he was a gunslinger? Or simply a hired hand?

"Ma'am?"

Grace looked up. As if she'd conjured him from her mind, the gunslinger stood before her. "Yes?" She blinked a few times to bring her mind back to focus.

"I'm done unloading the supplies. What would you like me to do next?"

She thought for a moment. "You've just gotten here. Do you want to settle in or get acquainted with the town? I'll be starting dinner in about an hour, and it's our pleasure to have you join us at the table."

Before he could answer, the shop door pushed open and Calvin came running in. "Ma! Everyone says you done hired a gunslinger!"

So much for keeping it quiet, Grace thought wryly. Was she to be the talk of the town now? "Yes, I *have*," she replied, stressing the correct grammar.

"This him?" Calvin asked, staring up at Mr. Clark. His eyes were wide with excitement.

"Sure is, kid," the gunslinger said, and grinned down at him.

"Why would a person like you want to work here?" Calvin blurted out. "There's a lot more exciting stuff to do than work in an old store."

"I understand there's a little excitement around here," the gunslinger answered, crossing his arms as he looked down at her son. "That's why I'm here. Someone's been stealing from your mother's store, and I'm going to find out who."

Alice ran in then, her face red and tears streaming down her face. Grace gasped, "Alice, what's happened?"

"I'm never going to speak to Marty Smith again, that's what!" Alice hiccupped, and ran up the stairs.

Grace hesitated, looking between where her daughter had vanished, her son, who had just dipped his hand in a jar of stick candy, pulled out a fistful, and had run out the door with some of his troublemaking friends, pushing past the young woman who'd come in with a basket of eggs to sell.

There just wasn't enough of her to go around.

"If you trust me, I'll keep an eye on the store," Mr. Clark said.

Grace looked at him with gratitude. "Thank you, Mr. Clark," she said. "Inspect the eggs for me? Three cents apiece, if they aren't cracked. Actually, just get them all, in case Calvin is the one who damaged them."

He nodded his head. "Of course, I can do that. But I'd prefer it if you'd call me James, ma'am. Mr. Clark is my father."

His comment, for some unknown reason, made her smile. "James, then," she agreed. "But you must call me Grace."

"Grace," he said softly.

A shiver ran through Grace at the way he softly caressed each letter in her name. She backed away, then looked over her shoulder, giving him the smallest of smiles, along with what she was sure was a bright blushing of her cheeks, and followed Alice.

Alice was in her room, sniffling. After knocking, Grace pushed open the door and sat next to her on her daughter's bed. "What's happened?" she asked softly. She wasn't even sure if Alice would answer, being at that age where adolescents tended to share less with their parents who "didn't understand".

"Marty has been going on walks with Laura Bevel," Alice sobbed. "Even though he promised he'd be waiting for me."

Grace tensed. Had her daughter been having such serious conversations already? She was in no small part relieved, though, that Marty was seemingly no longer interested in her daughter, and instead, Laura Bevel, who was two years older. "Men can be fickle," she said instead, opting for a neutral answer.

Alice wiped her eyes. "I'm never going to talk to him again," she swore.

Good, Grace thought. But she didn't say anything, just hugged Alice tightly, sure that there wasn't much she could say that wouldn't make her daughter upset. "There's someone I'd like you to meet," she finally told her. "I hired a man to help around the store. He answered my ad."

Sitting up, Alice's face cleared. "Was it that handsome man downstairs in the shop?"

Wincing at the enthusiastic question, Grace nodded. "Yes."

"Will he be staying here?" Alice asked eagerly.

"He will. He'll sleep downstairs but have dinner with the family. Both doors will be locked between the shop and our living quarters, so it will be quite proper. Speaking of dinner, I'll need your help this evening. As it's his first night here, I thought perhaps we could make a special dessert."

Alice's tears were gone, forgotten just like Marty was. For now. "Of course," she said. "I'll get started right now. May I make some cobbler?"

"That would be lovely," Grace answered, standing. "Please do some biscuits as well."

As she left, Alice humming behind her while brushing her hair, Grace thought that it would be so nice to be young again, and to have all of life's problems solved so easily.

Chapter 7

James couldn't stop thinking about Grace's smile. It was everything he'd imagined, and more. It lit her face, and he found himself wondering how he could make her do it again. And again.

"More chicken?" Grace offered.

"I'm about to burst," James replied with regret. "This is the best meal I've had in a long time. You are both fine cooks," he said to Grace and Alice. He didn't miss Alice sitting up taller, even though she flushed with pleasure.

"What do you usually eat?" Calvin asked, his fork stuck in a fried potato.

"It depends," James said. He wasn't sure how much of his past Grace would like him sharing, especially with the boy as overly adventurous as he was, so he decided to be careful in what he said. "When I travel, as I go through towns, I stop for a bite when I can. The rest of the time, it's traveling provisions. Bread, jerky, hard cheese, apples. Those kinds of things."

"Sounds good to me," Calvin said.

"It's alright for a time," James agreed, "and far better than being hungry. But a hot, homecooked meal, made by a good cook is something I could sure get used to." This time it was Grace who flushed, and something about that pleased him. She deserved to be complimented and suspected it didn't happen often.

Alice brought over a cobbler, along with some fresh whipped cream. She served James an enormous helping, and he grinned at her, once he saw the blackberries oozing over the white plate. "Thank you, Alice. I've not had blackberries since my sister last made me a pie."

"You've a sister? Any other family?" Grace asked.

James hesitated. Then, he decided to tell the truth. "I do. My father's got a small farm in Colorado."

"My goodness, that's quite far away," Grace said. "You've traveled all over."

"I do," he agreed. "It's nice to have a chance to settle for a while. I'm looking forward to being here." James tucked into the cobbler. His eyes closed for a moment as the berries burst their flavor into his mouth. "Mm, mm! This is good," he said.

"I'll make another soon," Alice promised.

James tipped an invisible hat to her, as his mouth was full, and the conversation turned to what the children had done in school that day. As he lost himself in their chatter, he felt relaxed. Content.

It would be easy to lose himself here. To pretend, even for a little while, that this family was his family.

But having a family wasn't likely to be something he'd ever have. Not many women wanted to marry a gunslinger. Even if it wasn't true, they'd be worried someone would be after him, putting them and any babies they had in harm's way.

Would Grace be different, he wondered as he studied her for a moment. He wasn't sure. She'd accepted him though, right into her home, and at her table. It meant a lot to him, and he hoped he could repay her. Catching that thief was top on his list.

Next was continuing to make her smile.

Chapter 8

Grace snuggled into her bed. It had been an enjoyable evening, with Mr. Cl—with James at the table. He'd shared stories, appropriate, no less, but also been so full of genuine compliments about the food, she knew she couldn't wait to prepare another meal for him. The poor man was obviously sorely missing homecooked food.

He was serious about his job too. After dinner, he'd asked her to take him through the shop, showing her where the thieves tended to strike. He'd asked a lot of questions, each of them detailed, and he'd even knelt down and inspected the floor, around the windows, the doors, and everything else.

She had almost laughed; he seemed part Pinkerton in that moment, with his determination to find something, but if he had, he hadn't told her what he saw.

With a sigh, she sat up, shook her pillow to make it fluffier, and then laid back again. She couldn't fall asleep. Not yet. It was her routine to check on the children, and make sure they were still in bed.

But...perhaps tonight, with Mr...James. She had to remember to call him James. Perhaps with him here, they'd behave. For just one night.

She tiptoed over to their rooms and was relieved to see both Alice and Calvin fast asleep. Returning to her bed, she nearly collapsed into sleep.

Morning came all too soon, as it usually did. Tiredly she got up, woke the children, and started breakfast. Soon, grits were bubbling, eggs were frying, and a slab of bacon was sizzling. It was a large breakfast, but she liked to make sure the children had plenty. With running the store all day, there wasn't time to make lunch, so leftovers from the night before, or from breakfast, were everyone's lunch.

Grace had just finished putting two loaves of bread dough in a pan to rise when there was a knock at the door separating the living quarters from the store. "Come in," she called.

A moment later, James's head peered around. "Good morning," he said.

"Good morning," she returned. "Come on in. You are welcome here at any time," she told him.

As he approached the kitchen, she pointed to the table. "Help yourself. The children will be here any moment."

No sooner had she spoken, then Calvin came out, rubbing sleep from his eyes but dressed in his school clothes. Alice was wearing her second-best dress, and had put a ribbon in her hair. Grace decided not to say anything, even though she wondered who her daughter was dressing up for.

The four of them ate, and Grace packed two lunch pails. "James, be sure to come up here for some lunch later," Grace said. "There is a little left from last night, and then bread, cheese, jams, and butter. Lunches are simple because I have to stay downstairs most of the day."

"After this feast, I'd be fine with bread and water," James grinned at her.

Grace ducked her head. She liked his smiles. They were infectious, she realized, as one formed on her face. She also liked having him around. Even though it had only been a day, it was such a relief to have him there.

"Did you hear anything last night?" she asked.

"No, and I went and checked a few times. Everything was quiet."

Grace nodded. "That's typically how it is. Nothing for a few days, and then something." She bit her lip. "I'm sure glad you are here."

He looked at her then, and the way his eyes burned into her set her stomach tingling. "I'm happy to stay as long as you need me."

Grace was saved from answering as the children accepted their lunchpails.

"Someone's out front," Calvin called.

She checked the time. "Goodness. I need to get the store open." Grace went downstairs quickly and unlocked the door. The morning was spent helping customers and putting out new stock. James was a tremendous help with that, and more than once she found herself sneaking glances at him.

He'd offered to stay as long as she needed him. While she wasn't one to take advantage of a person, and she *was* paying him, a small thought fluttered in the back of her mind.

Grace hoped she'd always need him. If he stayed forever, that would be just fine with her.

Chapter 9

James yawned and stretched out on his mattress. In some ways, working for Grace was a little harder than his usual line of business. For one, it was much more physically demanding. If he kept this up, his long, lean muscles were going to get a little bulky from slinging all those sacks of flour and beans. As it was, his back was already aching slightly.

He'd been there about two weeks. So far, everything had been quiet. In fact, almost too quiet, and he didn't trust it. From the dark circles under Grace's eyes, she didn't either. Things were going well, too well, she'd told him when the children were at school. When he'd pressed, asking about the yawns she kept giving, she admitted that she had trouble sleeping. She'd peer out the window often, checking to see if she saw anything lurking about.

That's why he was tired too. Determined to help her, his already light sleeping habit was put to the test. He barely dozed between checking the doors and the windows every few hours of the night.

He almost didn't mind because it gave him more time to think about Grace. She wasn't just beautiful and a good mother; she was smart, and funny, and smelled wonderful. Every now and then when he passed by closely, an incredible floral scent filled his nose. The longer he was there, the more he wondered how long he could stay. Part of him wanted to stay forever. Even if she didn't feel attracted to him, just seeing her, being near her, helping her...that would be enough.

The other part of him worried if he didn't leave, he'd fall head over heels for her and have to live with heartache. Something he'd never had before now, and wasn't enjoying the feeling of. Was this what it was like to have an attraction to someone? A constant feeling of discomfort and worry and unease as to what they thought of you? If that was the case, he was glad he'd been spared until now.

If he did leave, taking that heartache with him, he wondered how long it would take before it eased. With a woman like Grace? Maybe never.

The fact of the matter though, was Grace wasn't the only woman counting on him, and he needed to get more money sent over soon. He didn't quibble at Grace's pay—her meals were greatly enjoyed, but it was less than the bounty on a criminal.

A thought came to him, and James frowned and reached for his pocket knife. He flicked the blade open and inspected it. After dinner that night, Grace had come back down to the store to stock some supplies. He let Calvin use the pocket knife—with his supervision—to help open some of the crates, but he'd forgotten to see if it needed to be sharpened. Calvin had been so excited to see it, looking at it with full admiration, the boy had brought him down memory lane to around that age, when he had his own pocket knife.

Admiration. That was something he was full of himself. But for Grace. How the woman managed her home, the store, and her children was beyond him. It had just about worn her out though, that and the worrying about the uncaught thief. He wished he could ease her mind. He wished he could make her smile more often. The last few days she had been so exhausted, she hardly spoke between yawns.

James closed the pocket knife and set it near the dim lantern sitting on a stool. Maybe he should tell her he found her attractive. That he liked her. Wanted to know her better. Just as quickly, he dismissed the idea. Grace wouldn't want a man like him.

Sure, she hadn't said anything about him being a gunslinger, and she didn't mind the children around him, but at the end of the day, he was an employee. A hired hand. A man who was rough, dangerous, and not suitable for the husband of such a beautiful and refined woman. No matter how much he wished he were.

He pushed his hands through his hair and let out a growl. For a moment, he wondered. Could he change to be the right kind of man for her? But no, this was who he was. Trying to change who he was would be like trying to bottle up a tornado. Eventually, it would burst out and cause more problems than it had helped, to hide his true self away.

The only thing to do was pretend he wasn't interested in her. That was all. James closed his eyes. Sleep. That's what he needed. It would help him think better. He was too tired to think properly, anyway. Tomorrow, he'd start over, he'd feel fresh, and things would be better.

James let tiredness wash over him, and felt that pleasant heaviness come over his body as sleep came to call.

Squeeek.

The faint sound kicked his instincts into gear, and James bolted upright and reached for his gun.

Thunk.

Someone was in the shop. He eased his door open and crept forward. It didn't make a sound; he'd oiled it when he first came to ensure that. There was a rattle, like a key going into a keyhole.

"I'd stop, if I were you," James said coldly in the direction of the sound, cocking his pistol. The click was loud in the stillness. "Turn around real slow-like."

His eyes never leaving the shadowy figure before him holding a dim lantern, he added, "Turn up the light. Let me see you."

There was a suspenseful moment as the figure stilled, frozen to the spot. There was the sound of shuffling feet and the dim lantern swung a little. When the lantern finally brightened, James stared at the intruder in disbelief. "Alice?"

"Don't tell Mama," was the first thing she pleaded as she took a step toward him. Seeing the gun in his hand, she stopped and added, "And please don't shoot me, Mr. Clark."

James holstered his gun and took a long look at the girl. Alice was dressed up. Her hair was freshly brushed, and she was in her second-best dress. A glance at her feet showed her best boots, and around her shoulders was Grace's Sunday shawl. The one with lace and pale pink roses. He raised his eyebrows. Grace wouldn't be too happy to find her shawl taken without permission. It had been a gift from her mother, and something she cherished.

His eyes narrowed. "You are supposed to be in bed. Where are you going?"

A petulant side of Alice emerged. "That's none of your business. You aren't my father." She tossed her head and sniffed loudly.

It was true, even if she was mistaken in what she said, and James intended to let her know that. James shrugged and then hooked his thumbs in his waistband, one mighty close to his pistol. Alice's gaze followed. "I might not be your father, but it is my business. Your mother hired me to keep the place, and everything in it, safe. I suspect that includes you as well."

Alice's eyes filled with tears. It always amazed him how quickly young girls could get upset. "But you don't understand!" Her wail got louder. "If I don't go, Marty will forget about me."

Just then, there was a sound on the stairs. Grace came down, her robe wrapped tightly around her. "Alice? What on earth are you doing?" Then she saw James. "What's going on?"

Alice looked frozen. Her eyes were wide and she looked between him and her mother. Carefully, his tone even, James said, "Alice and I were just about to have a chat. She was going to explain to me why it was so important for her to sneak out, and then I was going to explain to her why it was so important she didn't."

Grace glanced between the two of them. James could tell she was wrestling with the desire to scold her daughter and to step back.

Alice wasn't looking at anyone. Her head was lowered, and her eyes were fixed on her shoes. When Grace caught his eye, he winked at her. She looked confused for a moment, then the expression cleared and she nodded.

"Well, then. I'm not needed," she said, and turned to the stairs. She paused, one hand on the rail, adding, "I expect my shawl put back, Alice Louise, and for you not to touch it again without my permission." Without looking back, she ascended the stairs.

Though he didn't know her as well as he'd have liked, James could tell that was a difficult thing for Grace to do. It made him respect her even more. She trusted him, and he liked that.

"Come with me," James told Alice, and pointed to the area of the store where several chairs for sale sat. "Sit here. I'll get us something warm to drink," he told her. "But don't you leave. If you do, I promise I'll come after you, and you won't like Marty seeing you dragged home like a baby."

Without waiting for her to answer, he went upstairs. Grace was pacing in the kitchen. Her anxious eyes met his.

"Just here for some tea, maybe some of that leftover cake," he told her. "Food calms some folks. Might do the same for Alice, make her talkative."

She nodded and had a tray fixed for him faster than he could have done it. "What are you going to tell her?" she whispered.

James thought for a moment. "It'll come to me," he said. "I'll fill you in tomorrow, if she doesn't."

He took the tray and went back to Alice, who was waiting, looking as though the end of the world was there. He motioned to the tray, and she helped herself.

James sat in one of the chairs near her. It was a fine quality. If he had a house, he'd want one himself. Maybe a complete set of them around the kitchen table. He glanced over at Alice. She had both hands wrapped around her mug and was staring into it.

"Well," he said, finally. "Start talking."

Alice wasted no time. "If I don't go see Marty tonight, he'll forget all about me," she said.

"So you already said," James agreed. He picked up his mug. "Now, explain why."

"Because...because..." Alice sat for a moment as she thought. "Because of Laura Bevel. If he spends all his time with her, he won't like me anymore."

"So? What if he does?" James asked. "Any man who'd forget about a woman he liked isn't worth having. Besides, you've got plenty of time to pick out a man. Being thirteen is a little too soon to start."

"I'm almost fourteen," Alice said, shoulders straightening.

"Give it a few years more. That's the time to start looking," James told her. "That's when you'll be able to easily separate the man you want to marry from the boys pretending to be one."

"What do you mean?" Alice asked. She tipped her head slightly to the side.

"What's Marty do for a living?" James asked.

"He doesn't do anything," Alice said.

James nodded. He had figured as much. To hear Grace talk, the man was nothing but a floater, living off one person and the next. "You like pretty dresses, don't you? And scented soaps?"

"Of course," Alice said. She sounded confused. He didn't blame her. He wanted her to figure out things for herself, not be told them, agree to hush him up, and get herself back into trouble.

"How do you expect Marty to buy you those if he's not working? What about a house, and a horse and wagon, and all the other things you'll need? How's he going to buy you those?"

Alice pressed her lips together as she thought. "That's true."

"Why, I'll bet," and James motioned to the small bundle set by her feet, "that Marty doesn't have anything, so he's always asking you to bring him something."

Alice sucked in a breath then. "He does," she said, and her eyes flashed. Her lips pressed together in a perfect imitation of her mother's irritated expression, and for a moment, James had to blink to be sure it wasn't Grace.

Alice reached down, picked up, and then opened the bundle by her feet. Inside were a few pieces of leftover fried chicken from dinner.

"Seems to me," James said, motioning to the food, "Marty's expecting you to take care of him. Not the other way around. It could even be because your mother owns a store, and so he thinks she'll be the one to give you all you need, and he won't have to do a thing but walk around with his hand out."

He let the words soak in. Soon, Alice was nodding. Her eyes were sad as she looked up at him. The anger had gone out of her. Instead, she wore a posture of resignation. "I reckon he does expect that."

"Now you just wait," James told her, leaning forward and helping himself to the cake. He pointed it at her. "You're such a pretty girl, you'll get to have your pick of anyone. But you pick one carefully. Look for someone always kind, always looking after you."

"Like you look after Mama?" Alice asked, her face now hopeful.

The question stopped him. James stammered, "What do you mean?"

"Like how you help at the store. And with the dishes and our homework. And make us all happy. Mama hasn't smiled like that for a long time."

"Well, I mean, you see..." James wasn't sure how to answer. Finally, it came to him. "Your mama is paying me," he explained.

Alice fixed him with a thoughtful look. "Not to help with dishes," she said. "Or homework. Or catching that mouse running around." Then her face lit up. "If you stayed, if you and Mama got marr—"

"Uh, let's stop there," James told her. "We aren't talking about anything but you, Jenny," he said, then corrected himself. "I mean, Alice. I'm sorry."

Alice looked at him then, her eyes curious. "Jenny? Who is Jenny?"

James hesitated. It was hard to stop his throat from swelling up from sadness. It always seemed to happen when he thought about her. He didn't want to talk about her, but he also wouldn't lie to Alice.

He cleared his throat. "Jenny is my younger sister. She was a lot like you growing up. Always feeling rushed because she didn't want to be passed over or left behind when the time came to find a husband. It got her into a terrible mess. She married the wrong kind of man. One who didn't love her, one who didn't take care of her. He used her for everything that he could get, and now she's paying the price."

"Can...can you tell me what happened?" Alice asked, biting her lip nervously.

James thought for a moment, then nodded. "Jenny is living in a boarding house, where she works far harder than she should, after her gambler husband lost their ranch and left her a pile of debts. A proud woman, she is determined to pay all of it back, and refuses help from anyone. She went from having the pick of anyone she wanted, to a single dress on her back and working fourteen hours a day, near worked to the bone."

He looked over at Alice. "That's not something I'd want to see you experience. It's a hard life. No joy in it. No opportunities for anything better, either."

"And she doesn't have anyone at all to help her?" Alice asked. "That's so terrible."

"I do what I can, send her money, but that's between us. She wouldn't want anyone to know she couldn't manage on her own." James sighed. "She's miserable, and sometimes I wonder if our folks had been a little stricter, if she'd have found a better man and been a different woman today."

They were both quiet for a moment, until Alice remarked, "I sure can't see Calvin helping me if I needed it, like you do your sister. So, I think...I think I'm going to be careful. What's the rush? I think I'd rather have the men chasing me, when the time comes, instead of the other way around."

She was quiet a moment longer, then added, "I know I've upset Mama. And worried her. I don't mean to. Not with all she's had to worry about with the store and Calvin. I added to that, and I wish I hadn't. I didn't think about how this would hurt her too."

She stood then, and hugged him tightly. "Thank you. I'm sure glad you are here." As she stepped back, she added, "You think you could stay a while? Maybe even...maybe even you and Mama get married?"

Before James could loosen his frozen tongue, Alice was on the stairs. "Goodnight!" she called, leaving him with the tea tray, the fried chicken, and a question that he suspected would be haunting him all night long.

Chapter 10

"Mama?"

Grace's eyes flew open as her prayer was interrupted, and she sat up. "Alice?"

Lighting the lamp next to her bed, she looked at her daughter. "Is everything okay?"

Alice shook her head. "Not really. I'm sorry, Mama."

Grace's heart started to pound. What had happened? She should have never gone back upstairs. Before she could ask, Alice was talking.

"Mr. Clark made me realize how I'd been making a fool of myself, and worrying you when I shouldn't have. Do you know, I think that Marty Smith only likes me for what I can do for him. Not for who I am. Talking to Mr. Clark made me realize I'm always the one doing things, like taking him food, or paying for something. He doesn't ever do that for me. Laura Bevel is welcome to him. I'm going to wait a while, see who grows up to be the kind of man good enough to take care of me, and who stays a boy."

Alice turned then to leave. "Goodnight, Mama. I'm sorry I worried you so much. I won't be doing that anymore."

"Wait," Grace said, and got out of her bed. She hugged Alice tightly. "I love you, Alice."

"I love you too, Mama." Alice pulled back. "I'm sure glad Mr. Clark is here. I don't want him leaving anytime soon."

She left then, but her words seemed to float on the air. "Neither do I," Grace whispered. And it was true. Somewhere along the way, she'd grown used to having him around. Would it be so bad if he stayed forever?

But the moment she thought that, she sighed. A handsome man like him wouldn't want a worn-out woman like her.

***

Grace smiled as she watched Alice walking to school with the other girls. Once she could no longer see her, she went back into the store. James was leaning against the counter, looking over a packing list that had come with a carton. A smile pricked at her lips as she watched him squinting at it, marking items off with a pencil.

"James," she said, as she moved closer. "Thank you. Whatever you told Alice, well...just thank you," she said.

He looked up then, and Grace's breath caught. His eyes pulled her in, and everything seemed to slow. There was only him, and an incredibly warm glow.

"I'm happy to help you, however you need, Grace," he said.

She wanted to answer. To thank him or to turn away and start unloading the box of ribbon waiting for her, but she couldn't. She just couldn't look away from him. Some strange force seemed to pull her closer, and she took a step toward him, then another.

Finally, her tongue unfroze, and she said, "Alice has had a hard time the last few years." Her voice was soft. Breathy. She didn't recognize it.

James, if he noticed her awkwardness, didn't let on. "You all have," he said, his eyes never leaving hers. "Especially you." Slowly, his hand moved toward hers, and their fingers brushed.

Grace didn't pull away. In fact, she actually wanted to move closer. She whispered, "James—"

The shop door opened then, and Grace hastily stepped back. Glancing up, she saw Becky closing the door behind her.

"Hello!" her friend called cheerily. "Lovely day out."

"Yes," Grace answered with a smile. Part of the smile was she'd seen more of Becky since James had arrived than she usually did. Whether it was to check on her or to sneak peeks at James she wasn't sure, but either way, her friend always brought a smile to her face.

Becky went over to the fabric. "I'm making a new dress," she said. "What do you have enough of?"

"Hmm," Grace thought for a moment. "I might have just the thing for you. I got a new order of fabric in a few days ago. Give me a moment, and I'll go get it from the back. I was going to set it out today."

"I'll get it," James offered. He disappeared, and a moment later carried out six bolts of fabric, setting them down.

Becky gasped in delight, and took her time choosing before settling on a soft rose plaid.

"You'll look beautiful in it," Grace said, then giggled, "I chose a striped lavender for myself, and Alice a solid mint green. I'm cutting hers out this evening."

"We shall look stunning," Becky agreed. Then she leaned in closely. "How are things going?"

Grace reached out and squeezed her friend's hand. "Wonderfully. Do you know, he had a talk with Alice? He caught her trying to sneak out. Whatever he said put a stop to it. Becky, it was amazing. She came and apologized to me. I don't think I need to worry about her as much anymore."

Until that moment of confiding in her friend, Grace hadn't realized how much of a weight that was off of her shoulders.

"That's wonderful," Becky said, and hugged Grace tightly. She pulled back. "Maybe he can help with Calvin too. And catch whoever is damaging your store."

"That would be nice," Grace sighed, "but that's sure a tall order for one man. He is human after all."

"And what a specimen," her friend agreed.

Grace laughed, "Aren't you a preacher's wife?"

"And a woman," Becky grinned, "who wants to see her best friend happy."

"You mean me? With him? No, no, Becky, don't be silly." Flustered, Grace picked up the bolt of fabric. "How much do you want? A dress length?"

"No, let me have it all, dear. I might do a bonnet as well." Becky wandered over to the thread. "I'll just get another packet of needles and four spools of white thread."

Grace nodded and gathered the items. "Anything else?"

"Oh yes," Becky said, "but I'll come back another day. I can't get it all at once, or Egbert might faint!"

The women laughed together at the idea of the pastor fainting over his wife's purchases.

Becky put her new fabric into her basket along with the other items and waved goodbye. She nearly bumped into the sheriff as he walked in.

"Apologies, ma'am," the sheriff said, as he tipped his hat.

Grace looked up. "Hello, Sheriff. What can I help you with? Those tins your wife ordered aren't in yet. I'm hoping next week."

"That's fine," he said, letting his eyes drift around the store. "I'm actually here looking for James. He around?" He shifted uncomfortably.

"I'll go find him," Grace said. She wanted to inquire what was wrong, but the sheriff seemed anxious, something she'd not seen before, so she left quickly.

James was in the storeroom, shifting boxes. Grace paused for a moment to admire the way his lean form moved. If she saw him every day for eternity, she'd never tire of it. As if he sensed her, he turned and smiled. "Grace."

Without knowing why, she flushed. "The ah, the sheriff is here to see you."

"Is that so?" He looked surprised. "I'll come right out."

James followed Grace to the front of the store, where the sheriff stood. She went behind the counter and pretended to be busy with her ledger, but listened carefully.

"I hate to bother you. I know you've got a job right now working here. But we got word Mad Hat McGee's been spotted. He's on the outskirts of town, hiding. I'm getting together a posse, and could use a hand."

When James didn't answer, the sheriff added, "It's a one-thousand-dollar reward. Half is yours if you help me."

James looked across to Grace, who had given up the pretense of not listening. "It's your decision," he said, his gaze meeting hers. "I'm yours, if you need me to stay."

Grace bit her lip. It sounded dangerous. Very dangerous. That was likely why they needed an extra pair of hands. But she also knew that was a lot of money, and he was used to that kind of money. Perhaps relied on it, even. It was far more than she could pay in a day or two's work.

She summoned her courage over the unease in her stomach and forced a smile. "Of course, you must go if you want to. The sheriff needs you. Don't worry about us here. We'll get along for a day or so."

She didn't miss the relief that washed over the sheriff's face. "Meet me as soon as you can," he said. "We might make it back by nightfall, if we are lucky." Then turned to Grace. "Thank you, ma'am."

As the sheriff left the store, James stepped close to her behind the counter. "Are you sure?" His eyes searched her face intently, as if he didn't believe her willingness to let him leave so easily.

"Of course," Grace lied. "It's been quiet here. I suspect another day will pass with the same. They need you. Just..." she looked down for a moment, and when she looked back up, was mortified that tears clouded her eyes. "Please, be careful," she whispered.

Without answering, James reached one hand up and rubbed away the tear that fell with one of his rough fingers. "Your skin is like silk," he whispered.

Grace wanted to press his hand into her cheek. She wanted to press her lips into his. He must have had the same idea. His eyes flicked to her lips, then to her eyes.

"Grace," he said, at the same moment she said his name. "James."

One of his hands was on her waist, and he drew closer. Grace stopped breathing. She tilted her chin upward slightly.

Then there was a gunshot from outside, and James pulled back, his revolver in his hand. "Stay here," he ordered, and raced to the door, throwing it open.

Grace stood still from shock, her heart pounding. She wasn't sure if it was from the gunshot or his touch or the fact that they'd almost kissed.

Before she could decide, James was back, his weapon holstered. "Misfire from the posse," he said with a grimace. "I'd better hurry before one of them shoots their foot off."

He went to his room, and a few moments later returned with his bag and a bedroll. "Sheriff has a horse for me," he said, and looked at her for a long moment.

In three steps, he quickly crossed to her, raised his hand to her face, and brushed back a stray lock of her hair. Her skin warmed at his touch.

"Stay safe, Grace."

He was through the door and in the street before Grace could reply.

"Come back to me, James."

Chapter 11

James took a long drink from his canteen. Even though the sun had already set, it felt unusually hot out. He was anxious to reach where Mad Hat McGee was hiding out. He wanted to get back to Grace and the kids. Sending Jenny half of his reward money was just a bonus.

Jenny. He ought to tell Grace that was where he snuck off to after payday. To mail money to his sister. He realized that she might mistake that for him being secretive about another woman, and he didn't want that. Not if he was hoping to see if there was something between the two of them.

He shifted in his saddle impatiently. The sheriff had made them ride slowly, split into small groups so as not to draw attention to themselves.

It was a good plan, something he'd have done himself, but James was anxious to be done with it all. Right now, Grace would be serving up dinner. The kids would be telling her about their day.

For a moment, a smile teased across his lips. The kids. His kids. That's almost what they felt like sometimes. He'd never been a father before, but he kind of liked being asked his opinion on things. Taking care of them. Alice and Calvin seemed to like it too.

Calvin had taken to following him around, helping at the store or asking questions about gunslingers and the men he'd captured. Twice, he'd even played ball with him and a few of his friends, and once they'd gone fishing. The more time he spent with him, the more he saw how much the boy missed having a man around.

Alice's question about what if he married her mama replayed in his mind at times, including right now. What would it be like? He was sure of one thing, Grace would be the perfect wife. There wasn't a woman more beautiful or more wonderful than she was. He was certain of that.

"About a mile ahead," the deputy said, riding up next to him and bringing him back to the issue at hand. "We're going to take the last half mile in slow. Split up."

James nodded. They didn't need to tell him that. He had been going after men like McGee for a decade. In that time, a lot of things had changed, but one thing hadn't. Criminals all acted the same. And it was important not to spook them. A spooked person was unpredictable. Catching someone unawares was completely different. Usually they froze in shock, but someone wary or jumpy tended to be extremely dangerous.

As they got closer, the sheriff waved men in different directions. "Circle around," he called, pointing to men and the direction he wanted them to go.

James tied his horse a short distance away behind a tree and crept in on foot once he saw the house. It was nearly falling down it was so old. It must have been abandoned. There was a horse tied in the yard, which was the only thing, other than a dim glow of a lantern inside the house, that gave away that there was anyone there.

The sheriff made a signal to wait, and that's just what they did. Faint sounds could be heard inside the abandoned house, but James couldn't tell what they might be. There was no way to tell. Maybe McGee was making his dinner. Or maybe he had others with him. That's why they had to wait, to make sure they knew what they were getting into. If a man ran in, guns blazing without knowing what was inside, he was the more likely of the two to get injured or killed. Hours passed. No one came outside.

Soon a lantern, hardly more than a speck at his distance, came into view. Squinting, James felt certain based on the shadows created that McGee was alone. The sheriff must have felt the same, for he signaled with a low whistle, and the men crept forward again.

From the corner of his eye, James could see three other men sneaking up on the building, splitting up to go around the back. One didn't even try to move slow, another dropped his hat and fumbled around for it, and the other kept walking loudly.

He shook his head. They weren't doing a very good job of being stealthy. If this was the best the sheriff had, no wonder they'd never been able to catch the thieves targeting Grace and the other townsfolk.

One of the men tripped, and the gun in his hand fired. James groaned. Was that the same person who'd misfired in town?

The noise was all Mad Hat McGee needed. The front door burst open and he rushed toward his horse. Somehow, James was there first. He didn't hesitate. With a swing across the man's jaw, he knocked him onto the ground and had him tied before the rest of the men had rushed over.

Mad Hat McGee's hat rolled away a short distance and the sheriff picked it up with a grin. "You're nothing but efficient," he told him.

James just nodded his thanks at the compliment and pushed his hat up a little. The men lit lanterns now, no longer afraid of giving themselves away. "What time do you think it is?" James asked, peering up at the sky.

"Around eleven or twelve," the deputy answered. "Let's head on back."

The ride back went quicker, but it was still after one in the morning before they arrived because McGee had come to and had tried to escape twice.

As they rode into town, James shot a glance toward the store. He was sure Grace and the kids would be sleeping. But what he saw froze him in his tracks.

The shop window was broken.

A light was on upstairs, and the pastor was hurrying inside.

Chapter 12

Crash.

The unexpected sound started Grace. She sat up. *Not again. Not tonight!* She grabbed her robe. Things had been so quiet and calm for so long. She'd thought the thief had given up. But then she shook her head. Maybe they had. Why was she jumping to conclusions? Maybe it was nothing. Maybe James had knocked into something returning from the posse. It was entirely possible. The thought calmed her slightly.

In the hallway, Alice stood in her nightdress, her shawl around her shoulders and a frightened look on her face. "Mama?"

"Stay here," Grace told her. "I'm sure it's nothing. Probably Mr. Clark returning and fumbling his way through the store. He might not have a lantern."

She hurried down the stairs. There was a crack of light under the door separating the stairs from the shop. She relaxed. It must be James. He'd feel horrible at knocking over something, she was sure. What could it have been? She imagined he was trying to clean it up now, and smiled. She'd help.

Grace opened the door and froze. There was a clattering sound, and then several whispered voices. Figures seemed to run every which-way. Then, one flew at her, and she stumbled back as something struck the side of her head.

Instinctively, Grace put her hand to the spot. It felt wet. Sticky. She was...bleeding? Her head throbbed and her eyesight dimmed.

It wasn't James.

That was the last thing she thought before she slipped into the darkness.

Chapter 13

Everything happened in a blur. James remembered shouting to the sheriff, and then running across the street, the man hot on his heels. They burst into the store. Becky was coming down the stairs from the living quarters, tears streaming down her face.

Dr. Jefferson came down next, talking quietly to Alice and the pastor.

"What's happened?" James said.

Alice screamed, a terrible, wrenching cry and flung herself at him. "It's Mama! They came back. They hurt her."

James pushed past everyone and flew up the stairs. His heart was pounding, and propriety be hung. He ran into Grace's bedroom and saw her lying there, white as a sheet with a bandage around her head.

Dropping to the ground, he grabbed her hand. "Grace?"

"Shhh," Someone took his arm and pulled him back.

It took James a moment, but he finally focused on the face of the person. It was Becky, Grace's friend. "Let's go back downstairs. I'll explain what happened," she said softly, in the same soothing tone her husband used in church on Sundays.

James stumbled after her, torn between shock and fear. Along with anger at himself. If he'd just been there, he could have protected her. He should have never left.

Once he was downstairs, Alice came over to him again. James wrapped an arm around her shoulders. Calvin stood off to the side, his own face wet with tears. The doctor was still there, and looked up.

"Alice, can you put your brother to bed?" the doctor asked.

Alice nodded, and pulled her brother up the stairs. Becky closed the door behind her. James took that moment to look around. The front window was broken. A barrel of dried black beans had been knocked over, and a stool, one leg broken, lay on its side. There was a red tint on it, and James stiffened.

The doctor nodded. "Yes. That was what hurt her. Grace was in shock, she couldn't speak well. Alice filled us in a little. Evidently there was a noise down here, the glass window breaking. Grace went down, thinking it was you returning and you'd knocked over something. She caught the thieves by surprise. One turned on her, threw the stool at her, and struck her temple. Another inch, a little harder..." he let his voice trail off.

"Alice screamed, she had followed her mother down, and that's what chased them all off," Becky said, picking up the story. "When she saw her mother fall, she ran to the doctor's home, then to get us."

"What of Grace's condition?" James asked, his voice husky.

"She needs rest. I gave her a sleeping draught. I don't think she can expect swelling, but that's what we need to look for. Disorientation, blurry vision, those are also things to watch for. In truth, it's a far smaller wound than expected." The doctor rubbed at his face. "I wonder if that means the assailant was a smaller individual."

James nodded. It made sense. But what kind of lowlife would attack a woman?

"I'll come by when it's light," Becky said, "and sit with her. Grace might not like it, but the town will understand if the store is closed a day."

"And I'll stop by and help you clean up," the pastor said.

"No, I can manage," James said. He glanced at the sheriff, "Can you have some men posted?"

The sheriff nodded. "I will. The thieves never struck twice in a week, so the next few days should be quiet, but I can do that. Especially, I can make sure no one gets in until the window glass is replaced. I'll send a man to Parson's Corner for another."

James nodded. "I'm going to check on the children," he said, and led the others to the shop's door. For what little it was worth, the broken window giving full access to the store, he locked the door behind them, then went up the stairs.

Alice was in her mother's room, sitting in a chair. James wordlessly dragged another chair next to her and the two sat. "Where's Calvin?" he asked.

"In bed. Won't talk to me," Alice whispered, trying not to disturb her mother.

With a nod, James set his gaze on Grace. Calvin could manage by himself for the night. Grace though...

"I should never have left," he said and dropped his head in his hands. He didn't realize he had spoken out loud until Alice rested her hand on his.

"It's not your fault, Pa," she said. He looked up as her hand flew to her mouth and she turned a bright red. "I'm sorry, I..." Alice looked at her lap.

James smiled. The name had warmed his heart. Truth be told, he liked being called that. He could get used to it. Alice still looked embarrassed.

"I hope you aren't mad at me," she whispered.

"If I was your pa," he told her, "I couldn't be more proud of what you did tonight. You're a real fine girl, Alice, and a credit to your mother."

She looked at him, beaming. Then, the two sat quietly, until the sun rose and Becky came to sit by Grace. Alice took Calvin downstairs after she made oatmeal for breakfast. Silently, they worked to clean up the damage left behind in the store.

James slipped upstairs to check on Grace several times. Each visit, Becky shook her head at him sadly.

He was getting worried. If Grace didn't wake up soon, he wasn't sure what he'd do.

Chapter 14

Grace tried to move, but her body felt stiff. She groaned as the throbbing in her head let her know that she was, very much so, alive. That was a relief. It had been a worry that perhaps she'd not survived; her dreams had been so odd. Her next thoughts were of Alice and Calvin. Were they hurt? Her eyelids fluttered and she tried again to sit.

"Grace?" Becky's concerned face came into view. "How are you feeling?"

She wanted to answer, but her mouth felt bone dry. Becky seemed to realize that, as she held some cooled tea to her lips. After a moment, Grace felt better, and the thumping of her head had reduced to a mere banging.

"What happened?" she whispered.

"Do you remember anything?" Becky asked.

Grace thought very hard. "Yes. I went downstairs at the sound of a crash. I thought perhaps James had returned and bumped into something."

As if she'd summoned him, James appeared alongside Alice, Calvin, and the doctor. Her room felt crowded, but she wouldn't have had it any other way. An immense rush of gratitude filled her at seeing everyone. James slid between Becky and the wall and took Grace's hand. His thumb stroked the back of her hand, creating a lazy circle that relaxed her. She hoped he would stay there and not leave.

"Can you remember anything else?" the doctor asked.

Grace frowned. "Yes. There were figures. People. They started to run. One came at me so quickly I didn't have time to move. They picked up a stool and threw it at me. Then, there was blood on my fingers, and..." she frowned harder. "That's all I remember."

"Alice was right behind you," Becky said. "She screamed, and the people in the store ran."

"I'm sorry, Mama," Alice said. "I know you told me to stay upstairs. But I had a bad feeling."

"You likely saved your mother's life," Dr. Jefferson said as he unwound the bandage around Grace's head. "Alice is a very clever girl," he continued. "She ran and got me, and the pastor and Becky."

Becky smiled at her. "Mr. Clark was just a moment behind. He's not wanted to leave your side."

Grace turned her head then, seeking James. The motion hurt, and she let out a whimper.

"Shhh," James said, leaning forward. "Don't move."

She caught sight of Calvin. He seemed frozen at the door. Each time he looked at her, he looked away again with an expression she couldn't decipher. She was too tired to figure it out. Perhaps later.

"Bed rest," Dr. Jefferson said. "I expect you to stay in bed at least a week."

"A week? But the store," Grace protested.

"I've always wanted to run a store," Becky said lightly. "Mr. Clark and I will take turns managing the store while also taking care of you. I'm sure some of the ladies from church will be stopping by too, as will the doctor. We won't let anything happen to the store, or let you feel lonely."

James nodded, but he'd not said anything else. He just held her hand. It felt so nice, so comforting, Grace couldn't help it. She was so relaxed in his presence, her eyes felt heavy, and soon were too hard to raise again.

She was aware of the others leaving, and the delightful pressure on her hand eased, but there was a brush against her forehead.

Had James Clark just kissed her?

Chapter 15

James brushed his lips against Grace's head. He couldn't help himself. It happened almost by instinct. No one had seen; the others were partway down the stairs when he caught up to them. He wanted to kiss her lips, but he wouldn't take advantage of a sleeping woman.

The scent of her rose soap still played in his nostrils, and the caress of her soft hair against his face made him want to pull her close. There was nothing he wanted more than to protect her.

It would be a long time before he forgave himself for leaving her side. If he even could. Right now, he wasn't sure. Everyone left, their moods somber. Alice took up the broom, starting to hunt for any final shards of glass. James looked over at Calvin. He was staring at the stool, the one that had hit Grace, with a strange expression on his face.

James walked over and set a hand on the boy's shoulder. "Worried about your mother?" he asked.

Calvin didn't answer. He looked up, through the place the window used to be, then back at his shoes quickly.

There was a flash of movement beyond, and James got to the window in time to see several boys running down the street. His eyes narrowed for a moment as he looked between them and Calvin.

"Alice," James said. "Can you look after things here, and your mother? Calvin and I need to go somewhere."

The girl nodded. "Of course. Where are you going?"

"Just around town a little," James said. "We'll be back soon."

Calvin followed reluctantly. They walked out of the general store, down a few stores, and then to the front of the sheriff's office.

"Why are we here?" Calvin asked.

James didn't miss his squirming. "I want to show you something," he said, and pointed to some of the Wanted posters tacked to the front of the building.

They stood, studying the images of men and the descriptions of their crimes. James pointed to one. "Dan, wanted for stealing horses. Bobby, wanted for robbing stagecoaches. You know I went and got one of these men myself yesterday, don't you?"

Calvin looked at him, confused. "Yeah. So?"

James strolled on, and Calvin scrambled to catch up with him. "Did I ever tell you about what I did as a boy?" he asked. At Calvin's head shake, he led him over to the small creek that ran through town, picked up a rock and tossed it in the water and grinned.

"I was the smartest there was. Got into everything quick as a minnow. Got out of it too, slippery as a fish. Nobody could catch me," he said, bragging.

Calvin's grin was just as he expected. James continued, "It was fun seeing how much I could get away with. Throwing mud on my ma's laundry when I got mad at her for making me do more chores than I wanted to do, stacking the woodpile so it would tumble down when I didn't want to work. You name it, I suspect I did it."

"So you liked having fun, too," Calvin said eagerly.

"Well, I thought I was having fun," James agreed. "But one day, I took it a little far. Played what was supposed to be a harmless little prank. But it wasn't. Someone got hurt. Real hurt. I'm going to tell you the real bad part though," James said.

He glanced to make sure Calvin was listening. "When they found out it was me, because people always find out, I was given two choices. Take my punishment like a man or run away."

"Did you run?" Calvin asked. "Is that when you became a gunslinger?" His voice was eager. Too eager.

James shook his head. "Nope. My pa told me that if I was old enough to make all that trouble, I was old enough to be punished for it. It was right too. I also realized my punishment was done from a place of love. You know what would have happened if I'd kept doing what I had? Or run away and kept getting into trouble?"

Calvin shook his head.

"I don't either, but I have a good guess. More people would have been hurt, and eventually, that would have been me. I'd have found myself in the wrong place at the wrong time, or finally caught, and looking down the barrel of a gun or being hung. Folks don't take kindly to thieves of any sort, and even less to repeat offenders."

James shot a look at Calvin. The boy's eyes were fixed on his shoes. He continued, "That's also why I became a gunslinger. I want to protect others. It's my job, and I won't hesitate to stop anyone, in any way that I have to, who is trying to hurt someone else. That includes your mother."

He looked over at Calvin.

"I don't want to be hunting you down one day, Calvin. I know you don't have a pa to tell you some of the stuff you need to know. So, I'm going to make you a deal."

Chapter 16

Grace set her book down. She'd only been in bed for a day, but she was already tired of it. She wanted to get up, but almost as though someone were keeping close watch, if she even thought about peeking downstairs, someone visited her room.

It was nice to have the company, but she didn't care for the feeling of being helpless and useless. She also didn't like staying in bed. It felt strange, when the sun was out and there were customers to help and a store that wouldn't run itself. It hadn't been long since the doctor had left. Perhaps she could just—

"Mama?"

Grace froze from where she had been about to push back the blankets piled on her. "Calvin. What is it, sweetheart?"

Calvin stood at the doorway, a miserable look on his face. When he didn't answer, she motioned, "Come closer. Tell me what's wrong."

There was a long pause before he said, "It was me. I've been messing up the store."

A jolt of sickening surprise blasted Grace's stomach. It had been Calvin? She blinked at him, speechless. Before his words could fully register in her mind and her thoughts start to swirl, he continued.

"Me and the others. We thought it would be funny. And it was real neat to make a mess and not have to do anything about it. No one got hurt when we played tricks. At least, not until you did."

Grace took a moment before she spoke. She was angry. Hurt. In shock. Finally, she said, "Was it you who hit me with the stool?"

Calvin's head shot up. "No, I wouldn't ever do that. Not to you. I love you. I don't know who did it." Tears filled his eyes and started rolling down his cheeks.

"What made you decide to tell me?" Grace asked. She took a deep breath, still feeling in shock over his actions.

"Mr. Clark," Calvin said. "He guessed. He told me that I needed to take responsibility for what I did, and stop what I was doing before I got into the kind of trouble no one could fix. We talked a long time about things and I made a decision, Mama. I'm not going to be around those boys anymore. I don't want to get in trouble that I can't get out of. It's not fun anymore. Not when someone you love gets hurt."

"That's a good reason to stop," Grace agreed. "Is there anything else you want to tell me?"

Calvin appeared to think very hard. Then he nodded. "Mr. Clark said I didn't have a pa, so he was going to tell me things straight like one. Things I ought to learn from a pa." He suddenly darted forward, his eyes wide. "He's also made me a promise."

"What kind of a promise?" Grace asked. She couldn't help but be pleased James had discovered the person responsible for damaging the store, no matter how upsetting it was, but had also made an impact on Calvin's behavior. She just hoped it would last and he meant what he said about staying away from those other boys.

"Pa said...I mean, Mr. Clark said, that if I take responsibility for my actions from here on out, when I'm thirteen, he'll give me his pearl-handled pocket knife. Until then, as long as he's here, he'll teach me how to use it for good if you agree. Like for carving things. Careful like, of course." Calvin looked at her, seeking her permission.

It hadn't slipped Grace's notice that Calvin had called James pa. Was he missing a father figure so much? He'd never seemed to before. Or was it James? Had James touched his heart the way he had Alice's? And hers?

Though he'd only been there a short time, Grace had to admit their lives had greatly changed, and for the better.

She didn't feel lonely. There was someone to help ease life's burdens, to talk with and laugh with, to share stories. The children adored him...and he seemed to like her.

It had all happened so naturally. When had their friendship grown into something that could be one day more? How had he slipped right into their lives perfectly, like a missing puzzle piece to complete them? And did he even realize it?

Grace had so many questions. The way they'd almost kissed the evening he left made her wonder what more could be. But...was that just a single moment? Was that something that would fade?

If she was being technical, he'd completed his job. He'd caught the thief. Would he want to leave now? Continue his obligation to help his sister? James didn't know she was aware of him sending money to her, and that was something she ought to discuss with him. She just couldn't pay him what he needed to help his sister.

"Mama?"

Grace's head snapped up. She'd been lost in thought and Calvin was looking at her with a worried expression.

"Should I get the doctor? Or Alice?" Calvin made to leave.

"No, dear, I'm fine. Just tired. My head is still aching." Grace smiled at him. He still looked at her, uncertain. "Would you hand me my tea?" she asked, hoping to ease his mind by giving him a task.

Calvin nodded and handed it to her. "Is it okay, though?"

"Okay?" Grace looked at him blankly.

"That Mr. Clark teach me to use a knife proper like for making things?" Calvin's hopeful expression nearly broke her heart.

"As long as you are obedient, follow his rules, and stay out of trouble, then yes," Grace said. "Learning how to make things is always a good pastime."

Calvin threw himself at her for a quick hug, then dashed out of the room and thundered down the stairs. The echoing made her head ache even more, and reluctantly, Grace put all thoughts of getting out of bed from her mind. Instead, she closed her eyes. Without meaning to, her thoughts drifted to James.

In just the short time he'd been there, he had helped her children, and been a tremendous aid around the store. Each time she thought about the moment he might leave, she felt as though her heart would break. It was a physical sensation that she'd never really experienced before.

These thoughts were doing her head no good. Tiredly, she let her mind rest, focusing only on the ray of sun streaming across her room and her throbbing head eased. Sleep was beckoning, and as she drifted off, she wondered, allowing herself one last thought...

Had James really kissed her? Or was she simply dreaming?

Chapter 17

It had been a stressful week, and James was relieved when the doctor gave Grace a clean bill of health. It was obvious she was grateful too. She went down to the shop immediately, and had seemed both surprised and pleased at how he and the kids had taken care of it, and everything else, in her absence.

Things were back to normal, almost. Dinners were together in the evening, and afterward, he taught Calvin, very carefully, how to use a knife. First, they practiced skinning thick twigs, then he showed how to do small cuts on soft wood to carve away and make a shape. Calvin had his mind set on one day soon making his mother a small platter or cutting board, though he didn't want her to know just what it was he was working on.

Grace always watched anxiously whenever Calvin had the knife, and each time James or Calvin's eyes landed on her, she pretended that she wasn't worried. Instead, giving a smile that didn't quite meet her eyes.

That made him smile. Almost always, he brushed his fingers against her hand, or his foot against hers. She'd blush each time, and look away, but that didn't stop her from looking back at him again with lowered lashes. He wondered what she might say if he asked her to join him on a walk or a picnic. Just the two of them.

James stretched out on the mattress. A feeling of contentment had washed over him. He'd sent Jenny some more money this morning. She had to be about paid off on the debt now. That meant he could stop taking a lot of the jobs he'd been doing, if he wanted. He could stay here. If Grace would have him. He knew she could use the help.

But then, how could he stay there, looking at her each day and not having her for his own? How could he see her beautiful face across the room, across the table, so near to him and know that he couldn't do more than look and dream about her?

Doing that was enough to make any man suffer, and those pangs in his heart and his chest and his stomach had been causing enough of that as of late.

No, if he wanted to stay, to be with her, he needed to do it proper. Get a plan. Find out if she was even wanting to get married again, let alone to a man like him. Then do it the proper way, and ask her.

It was easier said than done, though. That was the problem. He'd started to ask her one day, just to poke around and get an idea if she ever would want to get married again, but his words seemed to stick in his throat. James felt like he was rambling. His words seemed garbled. Mushy. Stuttering. Very unlike him, and it was quite embarrassing, which made it worse. Grace had appeared confused, unsure of what he was saying, but Alice had rolled her eyes as she put her hands on her hips.

"Just get it over with," she told him, and walked past on her way to the door, like she knew exactly what he was trying to say. Sassy. That girl could be sassy at times, but it was pretty obvious she did know what he was trying to say.

He thought the words to himself. He'd been trying to rehearse them, to see if he could manage to say it out loud. So far, they always stuck for the fear that swelled in his throat.

Grace, I think I might love you. Will you marry me?

But that, no matter how many times he thought about it or tried to say it, never seemed right. Never seemed enough. Why was it he could track down any criminal without blinking, no fear at all inside of him, and suddenly start shaking so much he felt about to vibrate out of his boots at the thought of telling Grace he wanted her to be his forever?

Maybe it was because he'd never been serious about a woman before.

Serious. About marriage.

The word caught him off guard. He never thought he was the marrying type. Never thought he was the father type. But Grace, Alice, and Calvin had more than grown on him. They'd become a part of his identity.

The big question now, was did Grace feel the same way? Or was she content in her ways, too busy raising her children and running the store to even think about making room for something more in her life?

As much as James didn't want to think about it, that worry felt like a sour lump in his gut. Rolling over, he shut his eyes, also trying to shut out the thoughts that were going to keep him from getting any sleep.

One way or another, he'd need to tell her how he felt soon. But how?

Chapter 18

Grace stood atop the short ladder. One hand holding the wall, she stretched as high as she could. She still couldn't reach the tin of ointment that Mrs. Haney had special ordered. Frowning, she stood on the tips of her toes, willing the ladder to stop shaking. How had it gotten up there so high? She just needed a little bit more reach.

But just as her fingers brushed against the tin, one foot slipped and she tumbled backward. Her gasp was cut short as two arms wrapped around her and she landed perfectly cradled against a strong chest.

"What are you doing?"

Grace looked up into James's face. He wore a mixture of concern and amusement. "I didn't expect to come around the corner and see you climbing the shelves," he said, still holding her close.

Her cheeks pink, Grace wanted to defend herself. She also didn't want him to set her down. She stammered for a moment, struggling to clear her mind from his nearness, then said, "I was trying to reach something."

"That's what I'm here for," James said, his voice a quiet rumble, and his face inches from hers. "To help you any time you need me."

Before she realized it, Grace's eyes had pooled with tears. Carefully, James lowered her to the ground, and she pulled out her hanky.

"What's wrong?" he asked. "Did I grab you too roughly?" He searched her face.

"Not at all," she told him with a watery smile. "I'd rather you catch me than the floor. In fact, I'm most grateful you did. That's not it. It's nothing really. I'm just...no, it's nothing."

The door jangled, and a customer walked in. James gave her another concerned look and walked away. Grace took a deep breath, then smiled. "Mrs. Aston! More eggs for me?" She took the basket and chatted about the weather and Mr. Aston's health as she counted out the eggs.

As she set Mrs. Aston's requested purchases on the counter, the younger woman hesitated, then looked down, before glancing back up and biting her lip.

"Is something wrong?" Grace asked.

"Well, I know it's not any of my business, Mrs. Fletcher," the younger woman said, "But..."

"But?" Grace wasn't sure if she should feel concerned or irritated. Usually, when someone said it wasn't any of their business, they didn't really mean that. Was Calvin up to no good again? Or Alice? Or...heavens, she hoped not, had Mrs. Aston seen her in James's arms? She stifled the sigh of exasperation that threatened her.

The younger woman plunged ahead. "It's Mr. Clark, ma'am," she said. "The whole town is talking."

Grace stiffened, but before she could say another word, Mrs. Aston continued. "We all think the two of you are just perfect together. I know I shouldn't be so forward, ma'am, but have you considered marrying him?"

Blinking several times, Grace stared at the younger woman. "That...wasn't what I was expecting you to say," she finally said.

"It would be so romantic," the younger woman sighed dreamily. "He's a real hero. Why, he saved the town from that evil man, Mad Hat McGee, and he's brought others in for the sheriff as well. Everyone speaks highly of him and, if you don't mind my saying so, he sure seems to have brought a spark into your eye." Mrs. Aston's eyes were lit up brightly. "He's just perfect for you," she added eagerly.

Without saying anything else, she gathered her items into her basket and giggled, "Just think about it. Our town could use a man like him around, and I'm sure you could too!"

As she left the store, Grace stared at the woman's back. She honestly didn't know what to think. It didn't surprise her that James was highly thought of. She thought that way of him herself. But...marriage. Did others think he was one she could...should marry?

Before she could think more about that, James walked back in and, with a grunt, set down a barrel. "This okay, or should I move it?" he asked, one hand on his lower back.

A surge of guilt rushed over Grace. He was working so hard for her. Was she being selfish wanting him to stay? He also worked so hard for his sister, to help her, and he could make much more as a gunslinger. Alice had whispered that to her, for which she was grateful. James didn't want others to see his soft side, his sweet side, but she enjoyed every glimpse.

And it was nice to know those quiet and quick trips to the bank and the post office were because of family, not another woman. She had refused to let herself think much about it, but knowing the truth made her feel much better.

"That's just fine," Grace said, forcing a smile onto her face. Then it dropped as she bit her lip. "James," she said. "I've been thinking."

He turned to her and raised a brow. "What about?"

"About you," she admitted. "It's not fair of me to expect you to stay here, working indefinitely. You've done so much. For me, for the store. For my children. We...are enjoying you being here, but I feel guilty."

"Guilty?" James looked at her, a slightly surprised expression on his face. "Why is that?"

"Well, you've done so much for us, and I can't afford to do much in return for you. I've realized it's not fair for me to expect you to stay here indefinitely."

"Is that what's bothering you? I've enjoyed being here. Your meals, your company, the kids." James got a thoughtful look on his face. "It's felt like home. Something I haven't felt for a real long time. In fact, that's why I've been wanting to talk to you about something."

She didn't know what possessed her, but Grace spoke without thinking. "Does that mean you'd consider staying for a while longer?"

The look that crossed his face made her feel physically sick. James took a step closer. "That's what I've been wanting to talk to you about. I can't."

Chapter 19

The blasted door opened, right as he spoke, but James didn't miss the hurt expression on Grace's face. He tried to speak, to explain he was interrupted, but she'd already turned away, greeting the customer.

Rubbing a hand over his chin, James felt frustrated. Things had gotten complicated as of late, and he didn't like that. Part of the lure of the gunslinger life was the simplicity. Go where you want, do what you want to do, no more than that. There was no one to make you feel hurt or embarrassed or angry. There was no one to worry about or fall in love with. Everything was business.

Just how he liked it.

Maybe that was the problem. He'd let their business agreement turn muddled. And that was likely his fault. He'd enjoyed being part of their family, but lines had blurred, and so had his emotions. And then when Grace got hurt...was that concern for her he'd felt out of a place of worry because of those blurred lines?

James didn't know. But he did know the more he thought about it, the more difficult it was for him to find an answer. He felt confused. And upset. But if that was with himself or someone else, he wasn't sure. That's why he'd wanted to explain himself. Get it over with. Ask her now how she felt.

But of course, they were interrupted. And he'd lost the opportunity. James waited the rest of the day, but he didn't get a chance to speak with her again, and dinner was a tense affair. Grace had apologized, saying her head was pounding, and had gone to her room. James took a plate to his room, knowing it wouldn't be proper to eat with the children and their mother not there.

Work done for the day, and dinner sitting heavy in his stomach, he felt restless. Usually after dinner, he'd play a game with one of the children, watch as they did schoolwork, or help Calvin with his knife. He'd been helping Calvin with his math, but both children picked up something wasn't right, and were quiet, neither of them asking for help when they peeked downstairs at him.

With a heavy sigh, James grabbed his coat and went outside. Soon, winter would be appearing. The cold wind rushing through the plains made that clear. He'd better make sure there was enough wood delivered. Couldn't let the place get cold.

The thought froze him in his tracks, and he shook his head. Why did he care? That wasn't his job. He was just there to help around the place. It was Grace's house, Grace's store, her responsibility to see she had enough of what she needed. The decisions made about things were hers to make.

But it wasn't the truth. Deep inside he knew it. No matter how much he'd tried to talk himself out of the fact, it was plain and simple. He loved Grace, and he needed to let her know that. If she didn't care for him in return, it was better he know that now. Better the children know.

Alice and Calvin had experienced enough hurt in their short lifetimes, they didn't need more, not if he could spare them.

If only he'd gotten to tell her what he was trying to say when that person came in the store. It seemed like every time he was finally on the verge of spitting it out, speaking his mind, there was an interruption. But now he felt worried in a way he hadn't before. There wasn't much time left to tell her, and it wasn't just because winter was coming.

Just like his finely honed instincts when he was hunting a criminal, and how he knew when to strike and when to wait, he knew now was the time he had to strike for Grace. If not, he'd miss out on the opportunity.

Grace was a strong woman. Stubborn as all get out, and if he didn't remedy this right away, he wasn't sure what was going to happen, but past experience told him his target, this time being with her, was going to get away soon.

He wasn't wanting that.

Chapter 20

Grace pressed her lips together as she chopped potatoes and onions. She was angry. At herself or at James, she wasn't sure. It didn't really matter. The fault was hers. She'd thought so much about James, let herself get so comfortable with him being there, she'd likely misinterpreted his concern for affection.

The moment she'd thought he was going to kiss her had likely been all in her imagination. As she slid the potatoes into the large pot and added salt and pepper, she seethed inside. The simmering water seemed to understand. Her anger boiled beneath the surface too. And how long would it take before it rose?

Anger was much better than pain. The hurt that was inside of her would come out if she let it, and that was something Grace wanted to avoid. So, she crumpled it all up, wrapped it tightly in twine, and kicked it to the furthest recess of her heart.

There. That was better.

Or was it?

She really wasn't sure.

"Mama?" Alice walked in and set down the carrots she'd been sent to get. "Are you okay?"

"Fine," Grace said with a tense smile.

"Is this about Mr. Clark?" Alice asked.

"Alice, this is about none of your concern," Grace snapped, then immediately regretted it. She sighed. "I'm sorry. Please forgive me, dear. It's been...difficult as of late."

Alice nodded, but her eyes never left her mother. Instead, she folded her hands and waited. When Grace picked up the carrots, washed them off and started chopping them, Alice said, "He really loves you, Mama. I think you should give him a chance to finish what he was going to say."

Grace's head snapped up. "Were you listening in?" she asked.

"I didn't mean to," Alice said. "But I was in the storage room, looking for another pencil. I loaned mine to Sally Mills, and she lost it. But, Mama, I think Mr. Clark had something more to say before that customer came in. And I think that you should let him say it."

"Mr. Clark made his position quite clear," Grace said, dropping the carrots into the steaming water and adding some cream.

"I love creamed vegetable soup," Alice said, peering in. "Mr. Clark does too."

Grace stilled. She'd forgotten that. James had enjoyed so many of her meals, she didn't know if there was one she made he hadn't called a favorite. If there was, she was tempted to make it just out of spite.

Grace was about to answer when there was a knock at the door between the store and the living quarters. "Yoohoo? Grace?"

She smiled. Good. An excuse to stop talking—and thinking—about James. "Becky, come in."

Alice quietly left as the pastor's wife walked in. She held a jar of raspberry preserves in her hand. "I just wanted to drop this off for you. It was my first attempt, and it turned out rather well, I think."

"The color is beautiful," Grace assured her, as she held it up to the light. "You've outdone yourself, I suspect. Thank you, Becky."

Her friend smiled at her. "I hope you'll think so once you taste it. You are one of the finest cooks I know, Grace. Your opinion means a lot to me. And others."

Grace blinked at the compliment. "We will have some tonight," she promised. "Can you stay for a cup of tea?"

"I'd love one," Becky said. "I've been wanting to talk with you."

"About anything in particular?" Grace asked, setting two teacups, sugar, and cream on the table. After she poured, she sat.

"I just wanted to see how you were," Becky said. "You've been through so much the last while."

"I'm much better," Grace said. "All recovered from the scare and healed up nicely." She took a sip of her tea.

"I'm glad," Becky said, adding cream, and stirring her spoon around her own cup. "I've never seen anyone as worried as Mr. Clark was."

"Yes, well," Grace paused. How was she to answer that? She took another sip of her tea and tried to ignore the expression on Becky's face. Becky was watching her closely.

When her friend didn't say anything else, she finally sighed. "What is it you want to say about Mr. Clark? I can sense there's something."

Becky lowered her teacup. "Grace, I want to speak plain. We are good friends, and I love you dearly. But I don't want to risk losing that friendship if I do speak my mind."

"You won't," Grace said, reaching over and squeezing Becky's hand. "You are the dearest person I know, and anything you say, I know comes from a place of concern and love."

With a nod, and relief washing over her face, Becky said, "Grace, I think you are letting your pride get in the way, and jumping to conclusions about what Mr. Clark started to say."

Grace tensed. Why did everyone seem to think that? She hadn't been jumping to conclusions.

At least, she didn't think so.

When she'd first told Becky, over tears and tea a few days before, her friend had suggested she go to him, and ask him to explain what he meant. But, embarrassed at the idea of throwing herself at a man, she refused.

Her soul felt tormented. She was eaten alive and her heart ached. How was she going to do that? So much time had passed. And if it was really important to him that he be heard, he'd have come to her by now, wouldn't he?

Becky pressed on, "The poor man is miserable, Grace. Don't you see that? He's so obviously head over heels in love with you, but the two of you are both unsure what to do. He likely feels inadequate. A gunslinger, a man who has never settled down. Maybe even doesn't know how. A man who isn't refined and experienced in family ways. It has him both scared and uncertain about what to do. I can see it in his face."

"That's preposterous," Grace said. "Why, I'm—" And she stopped then. Becky was smiling at her, and her eyes were gentle. Grace took in a sharp breath as she listened, really listened, to what Becky was saying. There was no judgment in her voice, just truth. Grace lowered her eyes, letting them follow a tiny tea dreg that floated on the top of her cup.

She was just as much to blame as James was. It was true, she didn't know how to proceed, and she shouldn't expect James to be perfect in how he handled a potential relationship. Especially when he'd possibly never been in one before, like she had.

James had been nothing but considerate, careful, conscientious. He'd been mindful of appearances between the two of them or him with the children. He was proper at all times. That created a natural bit of distance. Perhaps he wasn't sure how to put that aside either, and express his true feelings. Especially if he'd never done so before.

Grace's eyes closed for a moment, and she replayed, as she had often, that dreadful conversation between them. But this time, she saw something more.

"Does that mean, you'd consider staying for a while longer?" she had asked.

James took a step closer. "I can't."

But his mouth was open. She remembered that now. He was in the middle of speaking when the shop door opened. The look on his face, it was filled with regret. With frustration. With something he wanted to say. That's why he'd stepped closer. She realized it now. Had his hands even been reaching out to take hers? He wasn't ending the conversation. He was trying to start it.

Grace hadn't seen that at the time. Instead, she'd focused only on the two words. *"I can't."*

Alice and Becky might be right. There might have been more he was going to say. There likely was. His mouth was open...what if he was about to say something like: I can't yet....or I can't until....or I can't unless...

She was wrong to think that James was completely unattached. Why, he had been helping his sister. What if he was thinking about her? What if... She took a deep breath. No, she needed to stop speculating. Wasn't that what had gotten her into this mess in the first place?

There were many, many reasons why he might have said what he did. And now, she might never know what the real reason was. Foolishly, she'd let her anger and hurt wound her pride and possibly cost something special. He'd never want to stay now. Not in any capacity.

"We really have complicated things, the two of us, haven't we?" Grace said softly. "Maybe I did jump to conclusions. Oh Becky, whatever will I do? I've quite possibly made a terrible mistake."

"Perhaps it's not too late to see if things can be salvaged," Becky said.

Grace sat for a moment, thinking. The wind blew, rattling the window. Winter was drawing near. She'd better make sure to order enough wood. Perhaps James could help her to stack it before he left.

Because he was sure to leave, after the way she'd treated him. It was time to apologize and accept whatever consequence came her way, from her foolishness and pride.

There was the sound of someone coming up the stairs, and a then a knock. "Come in," she said, and then froze.

James stood there, looking at her. "Grace, I wondered if I might have a word with you."

Chapter 21

"Go ahead," Becky said. "I'll mind your dinner until Alice comes back." She stood and picked up the ladle to stir the pot.

Grace nodded. "Yes, of course. Should we go downstairs?" she asked.

"How about a walk outside, if it's not too cold for you?" James asked.

"Let me get my shawl," she answered, and quickly left the room.

James met Becky's eyes, and she smiled at him. Her face seemed to hint that she might know what he wanted to say. Feeling uncomfortable, he was relieved Grace returned after only a few seconds.

"Thank you, Becky," she called, as they walked down the stairs.

They crossed through the shop and James held the back door open for her, then followed behind. Alice was smiling at them behind the counter of the shop. He only hoped he'd be smiling soon himself.

It was cold out, but it could be worse. It would be soon. It didn't escape him Grace wrapped her shawl a little tighter around her.

"Need to order more wood," he offered, by way of starting the conversation.

"Yes. I'll do that tomorrow," Grace agreed, and then they fell silent.

They walked along the street, their shoes making soft sounds on the wooden boards. Not many people were out this time of day. Faint music trickled from the saloon, and in the distance he could see some cowhands driving cows. James frowned, wondering how to start the conversation. How should he approach it? He opened his mouth, but closed it several times. He was startled when Grace's hand rested on his arm, getting his attention.

When he looked at her, she said, "James, I need to apologize. It appears I was making assumptions, and that wasn't right of me. I also asked a question, without giving you a proper chance to answer, and then got upset at the answer. That was wrong of me."

James led her to a large tree, where a wooden bench rested underneath. Once they sat, he turned to her. "Grace, I want to explain my answer. In fact, there's a lot more I want to tell you. But every time I try, every time I think about how to say it, it doesn't seem right."

He looked into the distance, frowning. Rubbing at his chin, he grimaced. "I never thought talking would be so hard."

Grace surprised him with a soft laugh. "Well, I think you do well enough. Do you want to try again? I'll try not to interrupt, I promise."

He turned to her, searching her face. She was sitting, her hands in her lap, and her face anxiously searching his. Hesitantly, James reached over and took her hands into his. "Grace, I..." James swallowed. When had that rock landed in his throat? He tried to clear it, and then clear it again. There was a light pressure on his hands, and he looked down to see Grace squeezing his fingers.

He covered one of her hands with his, then looked up at her. "Grace, about what I said. When you asked me to stay. The reason I said what I did was..."

But the words were stuck again. James stood, releasing Grace, and started to pace. Maybe moving a little would dislodge the words.

"You see, what I mean is..." James stopped. "I don't know how to do this," he admitted, and looked into Grace's face. "I don't know how to tell you that I love you. That if I stay, I can't stay here, like this. Seeing you every day, but not being able to hold you or touch you or kiss you or love you. It would be torture of the worst kind.

"I don't know how to tell you that you mean the world to me. That I don't want anything more out of life than you, and Alice, and Calvin every day. I want your kids to be mine. I want you to be mine. I want so much. And I want it all with you. I hurt inside, and I'm suffering in the worst way because I don't know if you want me at all."

James took a deep breath then, and looked at Grace helplessly. "But I don't know how to tell you any of that. Not in a way that sounds proper. Or romantic, like women want. I've never done this before."

Grace stood then and took his hands into hers. James was surprised to see the smile on her face. She stepped nearer to him, perhaps a little nearer than was proper, and it made his breath quicken. "I don't think you could have said it any better if you tried," she whispered, and then looked up at him, tilting her chin and inviting him closer with her eyes.

Drawing her close, James wrapped his arms around her. "Does that mean I can kiss you now?" he asked.

"Absolutely," Grace breathed.

James lowered his lips to hers, but pulled back before they met. "Grace Fletcher," he said suddenly, "Will you marry me?"

"James Clark," she answered with a smile, "I'd be delighted."

He moved into her then, and as they kissed, James knew that while he might not be hanging up his gunslinger hat permanently, he'd found something his soul had been searching for.

The woman he wanted to spend the rest of his life with. And there was nothing, nothing at all, better than that.

Epilogue

Grace looked at herself critically in the mirror. It seemed the entire town was outside, waiting for the wedding. "Are you sure this color suits me?" she asked Becky.

Becky smiled and squeezed her hands. "You are a vision of loveliness," she assured.

Swallowing back the tears in her throat, Grace nodded, then hugged her friend. She took one more glance at her cream-colored silk, the dress she'd labored over for the last month, and then nodded. "I'm ready."

Spring's flowers were blooming, tiny dots of yellows and purples and pinks adding color to the long, drab winter, and it was the perfect time for their love to bloom as well, Grace reflected, as the pastor stood before them. The winter had seemed to rush by as she made plans for their wedding. One that was simple, but still included the people of the town, because everyone enjoyed a celebration.

Near her stood Alice and Calvin, with wide grins on their faces, each also in a new outfit. James's sister Jenny was in the crowd as well, and Grace looked forward to getting to know her, and perhaps encourage her to move there.

Once they'd each said "I do" and had kissed, Alice and Calvin rushed at them. James had hugged them both and Grace at the same time, and she was overwhelmed with the joy in her heart at the love he had for her children.

No, their children.

James had promised they were as much his children as any others they might have together would be.

Grace believed it too. She'd never find a better man if she tried.

As the town celebrated their wedding with a feast like she'd never seen, Grace tapped her foot as a small band played. She could see Alice and Calvin dancing together, and looked up as James offered his hand. "Care to dance?"

Grace let him pull her to her feet, and together they spun around the grassy area in time to the trio of fiddles.

"It's funny how things work out," she said, looking into her new husband's face.

"I agree," James grinned. "I'll be the first to tell you, I never thought things would turn out the way they did."

He stopped and looked deeply into her eyes. "I was scared I'd lost you."

Before she could answer, the sheriff and his wife danced past. "Can you believe it?" the sheriff called to them. "A gunslinger for Grace! Sounds like the perfect story!"

Grace's lips curved upward. "I like that," she said. "I think I'm going to write it down. Turn it into a book."

James laughed. "Just be sure you make me out to be dashing and handsome and brave. Really talk up my adventures."

"Oh, I will," Grace promised. "And I'll make sure we have a *very* happy ending."

James winked at her then and spun her into his arms. "Just wait," he said, his lips close to hers. "It will be the happiest one ever."

Note from Author

Thank you for taking the time to read *A Gunslinger for Grace!*

Could I ask for one small favor? Reviews like yours on Amazon mean so much to me and help others to find my books! Even just a single line means a lot!

Want a FREE book?

Stop by my website to get your no strings attached **FREE book**. It's my gift to you, as a thank you.

www.sarahlambbooks.com

About the Author

Sarah Lamb is the mother of two boys and wife to a teacher. She spends her days writing historical romance in the beautiful Shenandoah Valley.

There are other great books in this series as well!

Find all the Mail-Order Papa books on Amazon!

Made in the USA
Middletown, DE
29 October 2023

41511024R00083